ENGLISH FOR THE
RETAIL BUSINESS

武藍蕙 編著　　Bruce S. Stewart 校閱

LEARNING PUBLISHING CO., LTD.

編者的話

　　由於經濟繁榮，外匯存底雄厚，台灣目前已成為各大百貨公司、專賣店短兵相接的戰場；而從事服務業，若想穩操勝算，財源廣進的話，首先必須要有一口流利的英語，以提昇服務品質，爭取各個階層、國籍的顧客。「**店員英語會話**」就是針對商店服務人員，訓練各種實務英語會話的必備指南。

　　本書有三大特色，協助您輕鬆自在學好英文。

一、生動的會話實況

　　每篇均有詳盡生動的會話實況，並附中文解說，深入淺出，配合國情，教您如何接待客人，展示推銷商品，並適時反應顧客需要，從「接待基本會話」、「迎客須知」、「推銷用語」到「說明場所位置」、「說明營業時間」，徹底結合生活與實務，讓您隨機應變，用簡單合宜的英文，達成圓滿的交易。

二、豐富的流行資訊

　　本書引進國外最新資訊，並附世界名牌商品一覽表，簡明扼要地為您解說百貨商店如何運用各種售後服務及專業知識，如**免稅、打折、換算、退錢、分期付款、廣播失物、電梯會話**等，與顧客取得更進一步的溝通，使您永遠掌握流行動態，信心十足地迎接百貨新紀元。

三、精彩的專櫃語句

　　包括各式專櫃，如鞋類、仕女服飾、領帶、珠寶飾品、瓷器、禮品、玩具、洋娃娃等專櫃，以及滙兌地點等，貼切實用，使您馬上學，馬上能講。此外，並搜羅各式商品**專業術語**、**商店用語**、以及**活用例句**，應有盡有，使您能完全進入情況。

　　本書融合了服務英語的實用性、活潑性以及專業性，幫助您迅速具備英文聽、說、寫、讀的實力。並將應對顧客的技巧與百貨業、店面、賣場、世界名牌等最新資訊，都囊括在內，是您求職、入行、在職、進修的最佳利器。

　　審慎的編校是我們一貫的堅持，但仍恐有疏失之處，尚祈各界先進不吝指正！

編者　謹識

目　錄

ENGLISH FOR THE RETAIL BUSINESS

ENGLISH FOR THE RETAIL BUSINESS

ENGLISH FOR THE RETAIL BUSINESS

學習出版公司　港澳地區版權顧問
RM ENTERPRISES
P.O. Box 99053 Tsim Sha Tsui Post Office, Hong Kong

翻印
必究

本書採用米色宏康護眼印書紙，版面清晰自然，
不傷眼睛。

Part A

接待基本會話
BASIC USAGE

1 May I help you ?
招呼用語

<　**會話實況**　>

在競爭激烈繁忙的商業買賣上，接待賓客的開門第一句話，通常是先問好，如：*Good morning, sir (ma'am).* 先生（女士），早安。這是**服務業**不可或缺的禮節，而 *May I help you?* 我能為您效勞嗎？更是相當重要的招呼語，可以取代問候，激起顧客的購買意願，以奠定交易成功的基礎。

Dialogue 1

S : May I help you, ma'am?
　　女士，我能為您效勞嗎？

C : Yes. Can you help me find a souvenir for my daughter?
　　能不能幫我選個紀念品好送給我女兒？

S : Certainly... How would you like this doll ?
　　當然。……這個洋娃娃怎麼樣？

Dialogue 2

S : Good morning, sir. May I help you?
　　先生，早安。我能為您效勞嗎？

C : That's okay. I'm just looking.
　　沒關係。我只是隨便看看。

S : Fine (*Sure*). ***Please take your time.***
　　好的。請慢慢看。

Dialogue 3

S : May I help you? 我能爲您效勞嗎？

C : No. ***I'm taken care of.*** 不必了。我已經有人幫忙了。

S : Oh, that's fine. 哦，那很好。

 Useful Examples
──────────────活用例句─‹‹‹‹‹-‹‹‹‹

① Good morning, sir. ***May I help you?***

先生，早安。我能爲您效勞嗎？

Good afternoon, ma'am. ***May I help you?***

女士，午安。我能爲您效勞嗎？

② Please ***take your time.*** 請慢慢看。

③ As you please. 如您所願。

④ I'm just looking. 我只是看一看。

I'm just ***having a look.*** 我只是看一看。

⑤ I'm (already being) ***taken care of.*** 我已經有人幫忙了。

(= I'm being helped.)

⑥ What can I do for you? 我能爲您做些什麼嗎？

⑦ ***Is there anything*** I can do for you?

有什麼事情我可以爲您效勞的嗎？

⑧ Can I be ***of any assistance?*** 我能幫助您嗎？

⑨ Have you been ***waited on?*** 要我效勞嗎？

【註】────────────────◆◆

souvenir〔'suvə,nɪr〕n. 紀念品　　***take one's time*** 慢慢做

take care of 照料　　***have a look*** 觀賞；看看

Pardon me？
聽不懂時應付之道

―＜會話實況＞―

　　學會並熟練幾句打招呼的用語之後，如果遇到聽不懂外國人在說些什麼的情況，就必須懂得如何**客氣的周旋**，如最常用到的：*Pardon me?* 請再說一次。並請懂英文的人來應付。但請儘量避免在聽不懂客人所說的話時**笑嘻嘻**的樣子，因爲第一，這樣是相當沒有禮貌的，第二，在這段時間裏等於全然無視顧客的存在。

Dialogue 1： *C* = Customer 顧客　　*S* = Sales Clerk 售貨員

C : Can you suggest an attractive gift for my sister-in-law?
　　我想送我嫂嫂（弟媳）一個別緻點的禮物，你可不可以給我一些建議？

S : *Pardon*? 請再說一遍好嗎？

C :（*He says it again.*）（顧客再說一次。）

S : I'm sorry, *I didn't understand you*. Please wait a moment.
　　抱歉，我不明白你的意思，請稍等一下。

Dialogue 2

S : Can I help you? 我能爲您效勞嗎？

C : Yes, I'd like to buy some Christmas gifts.
　　是的，我想買一些聖誕禮物。

S : Well. *Would you please say it again*?
　　嗯，請您再說一次好嗎？

C : O.K. I want to buy some gifts for Christmas time.
好的，我要買一些聖誕禮物。

S : I see. This new perfume " Intimate " *is very popular with*
the young set nowadays. Maybe you can consider it.
我懂了。目前，這種新出品的香水 " 親密 " 很受年輕一輩的喜愛。
您可以考慮看看。

Dialogue 3

C : Please *direct* me *to* the grocery department.
請告訴我雜貨部在那裏。

S : *Pardon me*? 請您再說一遍。

C : I'd like to buy two loaves of brown bread, a pound of ba-
con, and a ham. And will you tell me where I can buy these
items？ 我要買兩節黑麵包，一磅醃肉和一條火腿。你能告訴我到
那裏買嗎？

S : Excuse me. *I'm afraid I can't say it in English.* Just a
monent, please. 抱歉，我不會用英語表達，請稍候。

 Useful Examples
活用例句

① That's fine. *I'll take it.*

① 很好，我要這件。

② Yes, there are five in assorted
colors and three designs.

② 有的，有五種不同的配
色，樣式有三種。

③ Shall I show you *a sample of
each*？

③ 要不要我每一種都拿給
您看看？

④ This price includes expressage.

④ 這個價錢包括運費在內。

⑤ *It suits you fine.* I hope you like it.

⑤ 這與您很相配,希望您喜歡。

⑥ Pardon me?

⑥ 抱歉,請再說一遍好嗎?

⑦ I'm sorry, *I didn't understand you.*

⑦ 抱歉,我不了解您的意思。

⑧ *I'm afraid I can't say it in English.*

⑧ 恐怕我無法用英語表達。

⑨ *Just a moment, please.*

⑨ 請稍等。

⑩ I'm afraid I don't know.

⑩ 恐怕我不知道。

⑪ *I beg your pardon?*

⑪ 請您再說一次好嗎?

⑫ Excuse me. What did you say?

⑫ 抱歉,您說什麼?

⑬ Excuse me. *What do you mean by 'grocery'?*

⑬ 對不起,您說 "grocery" 是什麼意思?

⑭ I'm afraid I can't *explain it in English.*

⑭ 恐怕我沒辦法用英語解釋。

⑮ Is that so?

⑮ 是這樣嗎?

⑯ I see.

⑯ 我明白了。

⑰ That's good!

⑰ 很好呀!

⑱ Congratulations.

⑱ 恭禧您。

⑲ Yes, I can imagine.

⑲ 是的,我能想像。

⑳ *That sounds interesting.*

⑳ 聽來似乎蠻有趣的。

㉑ *That's a good idea.*

㉒ That's quite possible.

㉓ I quite *agree with* you.

㉔ *I have no idea.*

㉕ Maybe you're right.

㉖ I'm afraid that's impossible.

㉗ Excuse me?
I'm sorry?

㉘ *Would you please say it again?*

㉙ *Would you please speak more slowly?*

㉑ 好主意。

㉒ 真是不可能！

㉓ 我完全同意您。

㉔ 我不知道。

㉕ 也許您是對的。

㉖ 恐怕這是不可能的。

㉗ 對不起？
抱歉？

㉘ 可否請您再說一次？

㉙ 可否請您講慢一點？

【註】

perfume〔'pɝfjum〕*n.* 香水；香味；花的芬芳
intimate〔'ɪntəmɪt〕*adj.* 親密的；熟稔的
set〔sɛt〕*n.* 一班志趣相投的人
grocery〔'grosəɪ〕*n.* 食品雜貨（店）（業）
loaves〔lovz〕*n., pl.* of loaf 條
bacon〔'bekən〕*n.* 醃薰的猪肉　　ham〔hæm〕*n.* 火腿
assorted〔ə'sɔrtɪd〕*adj.* 雜集的；各色俱備的
sample〔'sæmpḷ〕*n.* 樣品；樣本
expressage〔ɛks'prɛsɪdʒ〕*n.* 捷運（之費用）；快遞（費）
congratulation〔kən,grætʃə'leʃən〕*n.* 祝賀；慶賀；恭喜
excuse〔ɪk'skjuz〕*v.* 原諒　〔ɪk'skjus〕*n.* 藉口
moment〔'momənt〕*n.* 片刻；重要

購物流行語

- *lemon* 瑕疵品
- *It's a good deal.* 很合算。
- *After you.* 您先請。
- *Have a good time!* 祝您愉快。
- *Yes, please.* 好的，謝謝。
- *something new* 新的事物
- *You have been very helpful.* 你給我很大的幫助。
- *You can say that again.* 你說對了。(＝You are right.)
- *the bottom line* 重點
- *happy medium* 皆大歡喜的折衷價格

- *It depends.* 這得看情況而定。
- *Let me see.* 讓我想想。
- *First come, first served.* 捷足先登。
- *Business is business.* 公事公辦。
- *Thank you for everything.* 謝謝你的一切。
- *How's business?* 生意怎麼樣？
- *Check, please.* 買單。
- *You bet!* 好啊！
- *Please hang on.* 請稍等一會兒。

迎客須知
PROPER TREATMENT

Would you like to try it on?
詢問及回答顧客的意願

＜會話實況＞

　　要達成**圓滿的交易**，首先必須了解顧客的想法，因此如何去詢問逛街者的心意，便益顯重要了，通常使用 May I (we)～? 以及 Would you like (to)…? 是最恰當的態度。接著拿出產品，問一句：*Would you like to try it on?* 您要試穿嗎？如果客人願意試穿，穿好後再問一句：*How is it, sir (ma'am)?* 先生（女士），如何？就萬無一失了。

Dialogue 1：*C* = Customer 顧客　　　*S* = Sales Clerk 售貨員

S：Will you ***try*** this ***on*** for size, please?
　　您想試穿這件合於您尺寸的衣服嗎？

C：Certainly. But I also want to try another color in this style. Can I? 好呀，但我也想試試別的顏色，可以嗎？

S：***Go right ahead, please.*** 當然可以，請慢慢參觀選購。

Dialogue 2

S：Good afternoon, and ***what can I do*** for you today?
　　午安，我能為您效勞嗎？

C：I would like a refund for this watch which I bought yesterday, ***it doesn't work.***
　　我想退還我昨天買的錶，它壞了。

S : Yes, of course, did you bring the *receipt* with you?
　好的，您有沒有帶收據來呢？

C : Yes, here it is. 有的，在這裏。

 # Useful Examples
━━━━━━━━━━━━━━活用例句→«««‹«««

① *Would you like to try it on*?

① 您想試穿看看嗎？

② *How is it*, ma'ma (sir) ?

② 女士（先生），這件如何？

③ Will you *try* this *on* for size, please?

③ 您想試試這件合於您尺寸的嗎？

④ We're sorry, *we don't have your size.*

④ 很抱歉，我們沒有您的尺寸。

⑤ Would you like to try our shoe department?

⑤ 您想在我們鞋類部門試看看嗎？

⑥ Would you like to *wait or come back later*?

⑥ 您要在這兒等或者待會再過來？

⑦ Would you like to *have a look*?

⑦ 您想看看嗎？

⑧ Would you like to *have a closer look*?

⑧ 您想近一點看嗎？

⑨ Would you like to *have it gift-wrapped*?

⑨ 您想把它包裝起來嗎？

⑩ Would you like a bigger one?

⑩ 您要大一點的嗎？

⑪ Would you like this one?

⑪ 您要這個嗎?

⑫ Would you like to *check it out* there?

⑫ 您要在那裏檢查嗎?

⑬ What kind of color (material) would you like?

⑬ 您想要什麼樣的顏色（質料）?

⑭ May I have your name (address, telephone number), please?

⑭ 請問您的大名（地址，電話號碼）?

⑮ *May I be excused* (for a second)?

⑮ 對不起,失陪（一下）。

⑯ *May I take your measurements*?

⑯ 我能幫您量身嗎?

⑰ May we give you the answer to-morrow?

⑰ 我們明天給您答覆,可以嗎?

⑱ May I speak to Mr. (Mrs., Miss) Lin, please?
May I ask *who's calling*?

⑱ 請找林先生（太太,小姐）。
請問您哪裏找?

⑲ *Would you like to have a seat*?

⑲ 您想坐下來嗎?

⑳ Certainly.

⑳ 當然。

㉑ This one?

㉑ 這個嗎?

㉒ Here you are.

㉒ 這就是(您要的東西)。

㉓ Go right ahead, please.

㉓ 請慢慢參觀。

㉔ Not at all.

㉔ 不客氣。

try on 試穿

refund 〔'ri,fʌnd〕 *n.* 退錢;退還

have a look at 看一看

gift-wrap 〔'gɪft,ræp〕 *v.* 用華麗之紙張、緞帶等包紮禮品
　　n. 送禮包裝用之包裝紙、絲帶等

check it out 查看

measurement 〔'mɛʒəmənt〕 *n.* 測量

take one's measurements 量身材;判斷某人之性格

seat 〔sit〕 *n.* 座位

Would you please take your shoes off in the fitting room?
要求顧客

Dialogue 1

C : ***Would you please*** tell me where the restroom is?
　　請您告訴我洗手間在哪裏好嗎？
S : Yes, it's on the third floor. 在三樓。
C : Thanks. 謝謝。

Dialogue 2

S : ***Would you mind closing the door behind you***?
　　您可以把您後面的門關上嗎？
C : Oh yes, I'm sorry. 哦，好的，眞抱歉。
S : It's OK, it's just that we're trying to *keep* the flies *out*.
　　沒關係，我們只是不想讓蒼蠅跑進來。

Useful Examples

————————活用例句 ❮❮❮❮·❮❮❮·

① Would you please *take* your shoes *off* in *the fitting room*?

① 請您在試衣間裏把鞋子脫掉好嗎？

② Would you please *refrain from* smoking here?

② 請您別在這裏吸煙好嗎?

③ Would you please *sign* your name here?

③ 請您在這兒簽名好嗎？

④ Would you please *print* your name here?

④ 請您在這兒將您的名字以印刷體寫下好嗎？

⑤ Would you please *change* your money *into* Taiwan dollars?

⑤ 請將您的錢換成台幣好嗎？

⑥ Would you please *make a down payment*?

⑥ 請您付定金好嗎？

⑦ Would you please give me (us) some more time?

⑦ 請您給我（我們）多一點時間好嗎？

⑧ Would you mind waiting *for a second*?

⑧ 您介意等一會兒嗎？

⑨ Would you mind coming with me to the cashier?

⑨ 您介不介意和我一塊去找出納員呢？

⑩ Pardon me. Would you mind smoking in the lounge?

⑩ 抱歉，請您到吸煙室去抽好嗎？

rest room 洗手間；廁所　　flies 〔flaɪz〕*n., pl.* 蒼蠅

fitting 〔'fɪtɪŋ〕*n.* 試穿　　**refrain from** 禁止

print 〔prɪnt〕*v.* 印於　　sign 〔saɪn〕*v.* 簽名

change into 換成；變成

pay down 付定金；付（分期付款的第一期款）

down payment 定金

cashier 〔kæ'ʃɪr〕*n.* 出納員

lounge 〔laʊndʒ〕*n.* 吸煙室；交誼廳

請您別在這兒抽煙好嗎？

3 Please.
請的用法

<會話實況>

> 對客人要常用「請」字以表示禮貌，「**請**」**有種種的表現**，並不是一直用 please，如：*Won't you sit down*? 您請坐。就是另一種表現。這些基本用法能讓您擁有圓滿的人際關係，但要注意務須配合以和善誠懇的表情才行得通。

Dialogue 1

C : Can I try this on? 我能試穿這件嗎？

S : Please do, the fitting room is over there.
　　 請去試，試衣室在那邊。

C : O.K. Thanks. 好的。謝謝。

Dialogue 2

C : May I bring my dog in with me?
　　 我可以帶我的狗進來嗎？

S : Yes, you may, but please don't *let her run loose.*
　　 可以，但請別讓它跑丟了。

C : I won't. Thanks. 不會的。謝謝。

Dialogue 3

C : I like the blue one. 我要藍色的這個。

S : This one? 這個嗎？

C : Yes. 是的。

S : Here you are. 這就是（您要的）。

Dialogue 4

C : Can I test it to *make sure* it works?
　　我能試試看它能不能動嗎？

S : *Go right ahead*, just press that button to *turn* it *on*.
　　可以的，只要按鈕就可以了。

C : O.K. 好的。

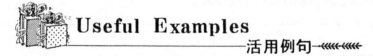

Useful Examples
　　　　　　　　　　　　　　活用例句

① *Go right ahead, please*. 請隨意去做。

② Not at all. 別客氣。

③ You're welcome. Please do so. 不客氣，請去做。

④ *This way, please*. 請這邊走。

⑤ Would you care for some refreshments?
　　請問您要不要一些點心呢？

⑥ *Help yourself, please*. 請隨意。

⑦ *After you*. 您先走。

⑧ Won't you sit down? 您請坐。

【註】

lost〔lɔst〕*adj.* 遺失的　　*make sure* 確定

work〔wɜk〕*v.* 運轉；工作　　button〔'bʌtn̩〕*n.* 電鈕；鈕扣

turn on 打開；發動　　refreshment〔rɪ'frɛʃmənt〕*n.* 點心

Shall I take your measurements, sir?
向顧客推薦

<會話實況>

　　顧客有些需要，如果我們能**主動提出**並加以解決，常能使顧客感受到週全的服務，此外，比較沒有主見或並無固定打算的客人，通常都會期望店員中肯的提議來決定購買產品的樣式。一句：*Shall I gift-wrap it*? 您要把它包裝起來嗎？十分有用。

Dialogue 1

S : Are you looking for something, madam?
　　　女士，您是不是在找什麼呢？
C : Yes, ***where's the dressing room***, I'd like to ***try on*** this dress.
　　　是呀，更衣室在哪裏？我想試試這件衣服。
S : It's right around the corner. 就在角落那邊。

Dialogue 2

C : This pair of boots is too big.
　　　這雙靴子太大了。
S : Here, try this pair on. ***It should fit you.***
　　　試試這雙，它應該可以。
C : It's still too small. 它又太小了。
S : OK, I'll get you a pair that's a size larger.
　　　噢，我再拿大一點的尺寸給您。

Dialogue 3

S: Can I help you, sir? 先生，我能為您效勞嗎？

C: Yes, where can I get this gift-wrapped?
嗯，我要把禮物拿到那裏去包裝？

S: **They'll do it for you downstairs**, sir.
我們在樓下有這項服務。

 Useful Examples
──────活用例句─◀◀◀◀◀◀

① Shall I *take* your *measurements*, sir?
先生，我可以幫您量身嗎？

② **Shall I gift-wrap it**? 要我把它包裝起來嗎？

③ Shall I put it in a box? 要不要放入箱子裏呢？
Shall I *tie a ribbon on* it? 要不要繫條緞帶在上面呢？

④ Shall I *check with* the maker? 要我詢問製造商嗎？

⑤ Shall we give you a call when it is ready?
當準備好的時候，要我們打電話給您嗎？

⑥ Would it be all right? 這個好嗎？

⑦ Would this be all right? 這樣可以嗎？

【註】────────────◆◆

dressing room 更衣室；化粧室　　corner〔'kɔrnɚ〕*n.* 角落；邊緣
pair〔pɛr〕*n.* 一雙；成對　　boot〔but〕*n.* 皮靴；長靴
downstairs〔,daʊn'stɛrz〕*n.* 樓下　*adj.* 樓下的
ribbon〔'rɪbən〕*n.* 緞帶；絲帶　　maker〔'mekɚ〕*n.* 製造者；製造商

We're very sorry for the delay.

如何拒絕顧客

<楼話實況>

　　百貨事務十分繁瑣，**常常有不能面面俱到的地方**，當我們無法達成顧客的要求時必須誠懇地說：*I'm（We're）sorry.* 抱歉。並說明原因，如 *I'm sorry, (but) we don't accept dollars.* 很抱歉，我們不收美元。

Dialogue 1

S : I'm sorry *we don't accept credit cards.*
　　　很抱歉我們不收信用卡。

C : Is a *check* OK then? 那麼支票可以嗎?

S : Sorry sir, we only accept *cash.*
　　　先生，抱歉，我們只收現金。

Dialogue 2

S : Sorry to have kept you waiting, but *I couldn't find the size you're looking for.*
　　　抱歉讓您久等，但我找不到您要的尺寸。

C : Can you order it? 你能幫我訂購嗎?

S : Yes, but it'll take about two weeks.
　　　當然可以，不過大概要花兩個禮拜的時間。

C : That's alright. 好的。

Dialogue 3

S：I'm sorry but *I can't give you a refund without the receipt*.

　　很抱歉，沒有收據，我們不能退給您錢。

C：Well then what am I supposed to do with this broken watch you sold me?

　　噢，那我要這只你們賣給我的破錶做什麼？

S：*I'll get the manager*, you can speak with her.

　　我會去叫經理來，請您當面跟她談。

Dialogue 4

C：Do you have any more? 你們還有嗎？

S：I'm sorry, *this is the last one*. We'll get the next ship-ment *in two weeks*.

　　抱歉，這是最後一個了。但再過兩個星期，海運就會送到。

C：O.K. I'll come back in two weeks.

　　好吧。我兩個星期後再來。

Useful Examples
活用例句

① *I'm sorry to have kept you waiting.*　① 抱歉讓您久等。

② I'm sorry, (but) *we don't accept dollars.*　② 抱歉，（但）我們不收美元。

③ I'm sorry, but this is *the largest one we have in stock* right now.　③ 抱歉，但這是我們現有存貨中最大的一個。

④ I'm sorry, but this is *the largest one we carry* in this department.　④ 抱歉，但這是我們這部門中最大的一個。

⑤ I'm sorry, but this is the last one we have *at the moment.*　⑤ 抱歉，但這是目前我們存貨中的最後一個。

⑥ I'm sorry, but we don't have any in stock at the moment.
I'm sorry, but they are *out of stock* right now.　⑥ 抱歉，但我們目前沒有存貨了。
抱歉，目前沒有存貨了。

⑦ We're very sorry *for the delay.*　⑦ 非常抱歉延遲了。

⑧ We're very sorry *for the inconvenience.*　⑧ 非常抱歉使您有此不便。

⑨ I'm sorry, but this is all we have right now.　⑨ 抱歉，但這是目前我們所有的了。

⑩ We're very sorry *for the mix-up* (confusion).　⑩ 這麼混亂，真是非常抱歉。

⑪ *I'm afraid* it's a little too big for you.

⑫ We're sorry we don't.

⑬ We're sorry we don't have it now.

⑭ We're sorry, this is all we have now.

⑮ *How would you prefer* this one?

⑯ We're sorry we couldn't help you.

⑰ Please call again.

⑱ Will you excuse me?

⑲ We're sorry to have troubled you.

⑳ I'm sorry to be late.

㉑ Excuse me *for being late.*

⑪ 恐怕它對你而言，大了點。

⑫ 很抱歉我們沒有。

⑬ 抱歉目前我們沒有。

⑭ 很抱歉，這是目前所有的存貨了。

⑮ 您怎麼會比較喜歡這個呢？

⑯ 很抱歉不能爲您效勞。

⑰ 請再打一次。

⑱ 失陪一下。

⑲ 抱歉帶給您麻煩。

⑳ 抱歉延遲了。

㉑ 原諒我來晚了。

【註】

credit card 信用卡　　check〔tʃɛk〕*n.* 支票
cash〔kæʃ〕*n.* 現金；錢　　order〔'ɔrdɚ〕*v.*, *n.* 訂購
manager〔'mænɪdʒɚ〕*n.* 經理　　shipment〔'ʃɪpmənt〕*n.* 裝船；所載之貨
in stock 現貨供應　　*at the moment* 目前
inconvenience〔ˌɪnkən'vinjəns〕*n.* 不便；困難
mix-up〔'mɪksˌʌp〕*n.* 混亂　　confusion〔kən'fjuʒən〕*n.* 混亂；混淆不清
prefer〔prɪ'fɝ〕*v.* 較喜歡；寧愛

Please have a look.
展示商品

<会話實況>

　　如果櫥窗或櫥櫃內已陳列出所賣的物品時，客人通常會**邊指邊看**，或請店員拿出產品，以便選擇。如：*Can you show me this*? 您能給我看看這個嗎？這種**直接面對面的溝通**，常能立即奏效，而達成交易。因此，此類展示商品的會話必須熟記。

Dialogue 1

C：(*Looking into the window case*) Can you show me this?
　　(看櫥窗內)能讓我看看這個嗎？
S：Certainly... *Please have a look.* 當然可以……請看看。

Dialogue 2

C：(*Holding out a photo.*) Do you have something like this?
　　(拿出一張相片)你有像這樣的東西嗎？
S：Yes, we do. Just a moment, please. I'll go and bring it right away.
　　有，我們有。請等一下。我馬上去拿來。

Dialogue 3

S：We have some others *with similar designs.* Would you like to have a look?
　　我們另外有一些類似圖案的。您要不要看看？

C : Yes, please. 好的，麻煩您。

S : Here you are. 這就是。

C : Oh, **this is much better. I'll take it.**
　　喔，這個好多了。我買了。

S : Certainly. Thank you. 當然好。謝謝。

Useful Examples
─────────── 活用例句→‹‹‹‹‹‹‹‹

① *Please have a look.* 請看一看。

② Would you like to *have a look*? 您要看看嗎？

③ Here it is. 這就是。
　 Here you are. 這就是。

④ *I'll go and check our stock* right now.
　　我現在去查看我們的存貨。

⑤ I'll go and bring it (them) right away. 我馬上去拿來。

⑥ Certainly. 當然。

【 註 】────────────◆◆

hold out 給予；伸出

photo〔ˈfoto〕*n.* 像片；照片 (= *photograph*〔ˈfotə͵græf〕)

similar〔ˈsɪmələ〕*adj.* 類似的；同樣的

design〔dɪˈzaɪn〕*n.* 圖案；設計

7 How much is it altogether?

交易

＜會話實況＞

　　舉凡商業買賣，最重要的籌碼無非是**錢**，因此顧客與售貨員之間的金錢交易是其中不可缺少的一環。現金、支票、找零錢及貨到付現（cash-on-delivery）等等都必須知道如何運用會話，來獲取應得的**利益**。如 *Here's your change of $200. Please double-check it.* 這是找您的兩百元，請數數看。

Dialogue 1

C : *How much do I owe you* for everything?
　　我總共要付你多少錢?
S : It's $5,600 *altogether.* Would you mind coming with me *to the cashier*?
　　一共五千六百元。您和我一塊去出納員那兒好嗎?
C : Sure. 當然好。

Dialogue 2

C : How much is it altogether? 總共多少錢?
S : *The total* is $2,000, ma'am. 女士，共計二千元。

Dialogue 3

C : Here you are. 這就是。
S : Thank you. Just a moment, please, 謝謝。請稍等。

Dialogue 4

S: Just a moment, please... I'm sorry to have kept you waiting. Here's your change of $200. *Please double-check it.*

　　請稍等⋯⋯抱歉讓您久等。找您二百元。請點一下。

C: Thank you. 謝謝。

Dialogue 5

S: *Here's your receipt, and this is your purchase.*

　　這是收據，這是您買的東西。

C: Thanks a lot. 多謝。

S: Thank you. *Please come again.* 謝謝。請再度光臨。

 # Useful Examples

　　　　　　　　　　　活用例句

① I'm sorry to *have kept you waiting.*

① 抱歉讓您久等。

② Here's your change of 50 dollars. Please *double-check* it.

② 找您五十元。請點一下。

③ Here's your *receipt* (purchase).

③ 這是您的收據（買的東西）。

④ Thank you. Please come again.

④ 謝謝。請再度光臨。

⑤ It's 100 dollars *altogether.*
　 The total is 100 dollars.

⑤ 合計一百元。
　 總數是一百塊錢。

⑥ Here is the money.

⑥ 請收錢吧！

⑦ Would you mind coming with me *to the cashier*?

⑦ 請和我一塊到出納那兒去好嗎？

⑧ Just a moment, please.

⑧ 請稍等。

⑨ *How much do I owe you* for this book?

⑨ 這本書我要付你多少錢？

⑩ Here you are.

⑩ 這就是。

⑪ It's $300 *for the first hour*, and $100 *for each additional 30 minutes*.

⑪ 第一個小時是三百元，而後每三十分鐘追加一百元。

⑫ Please *get* the ticket *stamped* when you make your purchase. *Parking will be free of charge*.

⑫ 在您購物時，請在票上蓋印，停車就算免費了。

⑬ If you have a receipt *exceeding* $300, parking will be free of charge.

⑬ 如果您有超過三百元以上的收據，停車就可以免費。

⑭ It is $500.

⑭ 五百元。

⑮ It is $1,000 per piece.

⑮ 每件一千元。

⑯ Thank you, it is $8,000.

⑯ 謝謝您，八千元。

⑰ Thank you, the total is $8,000.

⑰ 謝謝，總共八千元。

⑱ $200 out of $1,000.

⑱ 兩百元，收您一千元。
（找給客人零錢時所說的話）

《數字用語》

thirteen	〔θɜˊtin〕	13		thirty	〔ˊθɜtɪ〕	30
fourteen	〔forˊtin〕	14		forty	〔ˊfɔrtɪ〕	40
fifteen	〔fɪfˊtin〕	15		fifty	〔ˊfɪftɪ〕	50
sixteen	〔sɪksˊtin〕	16		sixty	〔ˊsɪkstɪ〕	60
seventeen	〔ˌsɛvənˊtin〕	17		seventy	〔ˊsɛvəntɪ〕	70
eighteen	〔eˊtin〕	18		eighty	〔ˊetɪ〕	80
nineteen	〔naɪnˊtin〕	19		ninety	〔ˊnaɪntɪ〕	90

＊唸到金額數目時，請注意英語的發音，重音不同。

【註】

double-check〔ˊdʌbl̩ˊtʃɛk〕v. 仔細檢查

receipt〔rɪˊsit〕n. 收據

purchase〔ˊpɝtʃəs〕n. 購得之物；購買

stamp〔stæmp〕v. 蓋印於；加記號於

Part C

推銷用語
SUGGESTIONS ABOUT SALE

How much would you like to pay ?
詢問顧客預算、喜好

─〈會話實況〉─

　　詢問客人的**預算**時用*How much*?是很失禮的，此時問話須有技巧，顧客才會合作地把預算說出來，接下來店員便可各憑本事，極力推銷客人所認為合理的價格範圍內最合宜的物品了。如*What kind of price range do you have in mind?* 您心裏的預算是多少？此外，有關禮品包裝事宜的問話也可依各種狀況，儘量發揮，有*Shall I wrap them separately?* 要我分開裝嗎？也有*Would you like to have it gift-wrapped?* 您要包裝起來嗎？或者*With a ribbon on it?* 在上面加條緞帶怎麼樣？

Dialogue 1

S : ***What kind of price range*** do you have in mind ?
　　您心裡的預算是多少？
C : Well, ***up to*** about $2,000.
　　嗯，最多二千元。

Dialogue 2

S : How much would you like to pay ?
　　您打算付多少錢？
C : Let me see. ***No more than*** $2,000.
　　我想想。不超過二千元。

Dialogue 3

S : *What's the maximum price you have in mind*?
   您預算的最高價是多少？
C : Well, I don't really care. 嗯，我並不很在乎要花多少錢。

Dialogue 4

S : Shall I wrap them *separately*?
   要我分開包裝嗎？
C : No, it's okay. They can be together.
   不要，沒關係。可以裝在一起。

Dialogue 5

S : Would you like to *have it gift-wrapped*?
   您要我把它包裝成禮品嗎？
C : Yes, please. 是的，麻煩您。
S : *With a ribbon*? 要緞帶嗎？
C : Yes, that'll be nice. 要，那會很好看。
S : Certainly, sir. 當然，先生。

Dialogue 6

C : Can you *wrap it for a present*?
   您能把它當禮品一樣包裝起來嗎？
S : Yes, certainly. Would you like a ribbon on it?
   當然可以。您要在上面繫緞帶嗎？
C : Yes, please. 要，麻煩您。
S : What color would you like? We have green, red, and pink.
   您要什麼顏色？有綠色，紅色，和粉紅色的。
C : I'll *leave it up to you*. 讓您決定好了。

 # Useful Examples
活用例句

① **What (kind of) price range** do you have in mind?
How much would you like to pay?

① 您的預算在多少的價格範圍之內？

② **What's the maximum price** you have in mind?

② 您預算的最高價是多少？

③ Up to $2,000.

③ 最多兩千元。

④ I don't really care.

④ 我並不擔心。

⑤ What kind of flower did you have in mind?

⑤ 您想要什麼樣子的花？

⑥ What types of ～ would you prefer?

⑥ 您想要什麼樣子的？

⑦ What kind of shoes are you looking for?

⑦ 您想要什麼樣子的鞋子呢？

⑧ Shall I **wrap them separately** (= **individually**)?

⑧ 要我分開包裝嗎？

⑨ Is it a present?

⑨ 是送人的嗎？

⑩ Shall I gift-wrap it?
Would you like to **have it gift-wrapped**?

⑩ 要我包裝成禮品嗎？

⑪ Can you wrap it **for a present**?

⑪ 您能把它包裝成禮品嗎？

⑫ I like it better with a ribbon.

⑬ I'll *leave it up to you.*

⑫ 我比較喜歡有緞帶的。

⑬ 由您決定。

您要把它當禮品一樣地包裝起來嗎？

range〔rendʒ〕*n.* 範圍；界限
have in mind 欲；計畫　　*up to* 數達；高達
maximum〔'mæksəməm〕*n.* 最大量；最高點
wrap〔ræp〕*v.* 包裹　*n.* 包裝材料
separately〔'sɛpərɪtlɪ〕*adv.* 分開地
up to someone 由某人決定

That color sure looks good on you.
建議顧客顏色、式樣

<＜會話實況＞>

　　顧客逛街購物，第一眼被吸引的大都是商品眩麗的外觀，如果店員能深諳顧客心理，對其喜愛的物品**加以忠實的建議**，*It looks good on you.* 它十分適合您。通常就能達到賓主盡歡的效果。但要注意的是，店員不可自恃英語流利，誇張語調，刻意迎合顧客，以免**弄巧成拙**，使顧客產生警戒心。

Dialogue 1

S : How are you doing? 怎麼樣？

C : Hmm.... **It's not bad**, is it? 嗯……不賴，不是嗎？

S : No, **it sure looks good on you**. 是呀！穿在您身上十分合適。

Dialogue 2

C : I don't think this kind of color **suits** me. What do you think?
　　我想那種顏色不適合我。你認為呢？

S : I think **it suits you well**. 我覺得它非常適合您。

Dialogue 3

C : Can you pick me one that **goes well with** this jacket?
　　你能幫我挑一件可以搭配這件夾克的嗎？

S : Certainly. I think this type of color is **well-suited for** it.
　　當然能。我覺得這種顏色非常適合。

Dialogue 4

C : I don't think *it's a good match to have this with that.*
What do you think?

我覺得這件和那件並不是好的搭配。你認為呢?

S : I think they suit each other well.

我認為兩者搭配得很好。

 Useful Examples

─────── 活用例句 ─◄◄◄◄◄◄◄◄

① How are you doing?

① 怎麼樣?(本句也是常用的問候語等於 How are you?)

② How do you like it?

② 您喜不喜歡?

③ *It sure looks good on you.*
It suits you pretty well.

③ 非常適合您。

④ I think this color (style, design, pattern) is *well-suited for* this shirt.

④ 我認為這顏色(款式,圖案,花樣)很配這件襯衫。

⑤ *It seems to me* that this tablecloth *goes well with* that kind of chinaware.

⑤ 我覺得這條桌巾跟那種瓷器很搭配。

⑥ I think this pattern *suits* this type of jacket.

⑥ 我想這花樣適合這種夾克。

⑦ *It's not bad, is it*?

⑦ 不賴,不是嗎?

⑧ What do you think?

⑧ 你認為呢?

⑨ Can you *pick* me one that goes well with this suit?

Can you *select* one for me that is well suited for this suit?

Can you *match* me this one?

⑨ 你能幫我挑一件能搭配這套衣服的嗎？

你能替我選件能搭配這套的嗎？

你能幫我配這個嗎？

suit〔sjut；sut〕*v.* 適合於　*n.* 一套（衣服）

type〔taɪp〕*n.* 類型；式樣

match〔mætʃ〕*n.，v.* 相配

tablecloth〔'tebl̩,klɔθ〕*n.* 桌布

chinaware〔'tʃaɪnə,wɛr〕*n.* 瓷器

pattern〔'pætən〕*n.* 圖案；花樣

jacket〔'dʒækɪt〕*n.* 夾克

select〔sə'lɛkt〕*v.* 挑選；選擇

I think it's a little too small for you.
建議顧客尺寸大小

<會話實況>

　　如果顧客試穿衣物，覺得**尺寸不合**，店員可在存貨中儘量取出適合顧客尺寸的服飾，然後說：*I think this one gives you a better fit.* 我覺得這件比較適合您。

Dialogue 1

S : I think it's *a little too small* for you.
　　我認爲您穿有點太小。
C : *I feel comfortable*, though. 但我覺得很舒適。
S : I'm afraid it doesn't look comfortable for a jacket.
　　恐怕它看起來並不是一件舒適的夾克。

Dialogue 2

C : Do you have a larger one? 有大一點的嗎？
S : Certainly.... I think this size will *give you a better fit*.
　　當然有……我想你穿這一號較合身。

Dialogue 3

C : Do you think it'll fit me? 你想我穿合身嗎？
S : *How big is your chest*? 您胸圍多少？
C : I don't know my size *in centimeters*.
　　我不知道換算成公分是多少。

S : ***Shall I take your measurements***? 我幫您量好嗎？

C : Yes, please. 好的，麻煩你。

S : It's about 92, so I think this one gives you a better fit.
大概92公分，所以我想您穿這件較合身。

Dialogue 4

C : You don't seem to have my size ***on the shelf***.
你們架子上好像沒有我的尺寸。

S : Just a moment, please. I'll go and check our stock. ***How much do you measure around your waist***?
請等一下。我會去查看存貨。您的腰圍多少？

Dialogue 5

C : I want to ***try*** these ***on***. 我想要試穿這些。

S : Certainly. ***The fitting room is this way***... How are you doing? (*She opens the curtain*) Let's see how much we can ***turn up the bottoms***.
當然好。試衣間在這邊……。怎麼樣？（她拉開簾幕）我們看看能把衣服下邊捲上來多少？

 Useful Examples
━━━━━━━━━━━━━━活用例句━◀◀◀◀◀◀◀

① It seems to me that it's ***a bit too small*** (***large***) for you. 　　① 我覺得您穿有點太小（大）。

② ***It fits you perfectly.*** 　　② 您穿十分合身。

③ ***How big*** (***large***) ***is your chest***? 　　③ 您的胸圍多少？

④ *How much do you measure around your waist?*

④ 您的腰圍多少？

⑤ It seems to me that this size will *give you a better fit.*

⑤ 我覺得您穿這一號較合身。

⑥ Shall I *take* your *measurements?*

⑥ 我幫你量尺寸好嗎？

⑦ Let's see how much we can *turn up* the bottoms.

⑦ 我們看看能把衣邊翻多少上來。

⑧ *I'm afraid* it doesn't look comfortable.

⑧ 恐怕看起來並不舒適。

⑨ I feel comfortable, though.

⑨ 但我覺得很舒適。

⑩ *You don't seem to have my size on the shelf.*

⑩ 架子上好像沒有我的尺寸。

衣飾專用術語

- **comfortable** 〔'kʌmfətəbļ〕 *adj.* 舒適的
- **fit** 〔fɪt〕 *v.* 合適　　　　**chest** 〔tʃɛst〕 *n.* 胸部
- **centimeter** 〔'sɛntə,mitɚ〕 *n.* （長度名）公分
- **shelf** 〔ʃɛlf〕 *n.* 架　　　　**waist** 〔west〕 *n.* 腰部
- ***try on*** 試穿（衣服等）　　　***turn up*** 捲起；向上翻轉
- **bottom** 〔'bɑtəm〕 *n.* 下面；底部
- ***urgent order*** 速件　　　***minor discrepancy*** 小瑕疵
- **stretch** 〔strɛtʃ〕 *v., n.* 可鬆可緊；伸展
- ***take in*** 收小　　　　***let out*** 放大

- **alteration** 〔,ɔltə'reʃən〕 *n.* 改動；修改
  （＝ adjustment 〔ə'dʒʌstmənt〕）
- **shorten** 〔'ʃɔrtņ〕 *v.* 改短（＝ *take up the hem*）
- **reline** 〔ri'laɪn〕 *v.* 換裏子
- ***replace a collar*** 換領子
- **sleeveless** 〔'slivlɪs〕 *n.* 無袖
- ***extra large*** (*size*) 特大號
- ***cuff link*** 袖鈕　　　　**zipper** 〔'zɪpɚ〕 *n.* 拉鍊
- ***petite size*** 小號

4 This is popular now.
説明流行款式

<＜會話實況＞>

　　向客人強調**流行**的設計及顏色，通常可以滿足顧客**求新求變**的購物心理，故此時使用最頻繁的用語是：*This is the most popular now.* 這是目前最流行的。

Dialogue 1

　　(*At the Designer's Brand Department*)
　　(在設計師名牌部門)

C : **What's his favorite color** this year?
　　今年他最喜愛什麼顏色？

S : I think white. **Most of his designs are not possible without white.**
　　我想是白色。他大部分的設計都離不開白色。

Dialogue 2

S : This is the most popular style this winter.
　　這是今年冬天最流行的款式。

C : That's okay. I don't care what other people wear... Let me have this one.
　　好。我不管別人穿什麼……我買這件。

S : Certainly. 當然好。

Useful Examples

活用例句

① White is his favorite color this year.

他今年最喜愛的顏色是白色。

② White is the hottest color this summer.

白色是今夏最熱門的顏色。

③ This is the most popular style. 這是最流行的款式。

④ I don't care **what other people wear.**

我不在意別人穿什麼。

【註】

designer 〔dɪˈzaɪnə〕 *n.* 設計家

brand 〔brænd〕 *n.* 商標；牌子　　department 〔dɪˈpɑrtmənt〕 *n.* 部門

favorite 〔ˈfevərɪt〕 *adj.* 最喜愛的　 *n.* 最被喜愛之人或物

popular 〔ˈpɑpjələ〕 *adj.* 流行的；受歡迎的

style 〔staɪl〕 *n.* 樣式；風格（衣服的款式用 style，而在電氣用品或車輛上則用 model 〔ˈmɑdḷ〕 *n.* 型式 ）

我覺得
它非常適合您。

流行物品專用術語

- *honey sand-grinding cream* 蜂蜜磨砂膏
- *eye-liner pencil* 眼線筆
- **essence** 〔'ɛsn̩s 〕*n.* 香水;香精
- *perfumed soap* 香皂
- **cosmetics** 〔kɑz'mɛtɪk 〕*n.* 化粧品
- **embroidery** 〔ɪm'brɔɪdərɪ 〕*n.* 繡花;刺繡
- **homespun** 〔'hom,spʌn 〕*n.* 手織物
- *shoulder padding* 墊肩
- **bangle** 〔'bæŋgl̩ 〕*n.* 手鐲;環飾;腳鐲
- **bracelet** 〔'breslɪt 〕*n.* 手鐲;臂鐲
- *coin dots* 大圓點花　　　　*pin dots* 小圓點花
- *man-made fiber* 人造纖維
- *lattice check* 小方格　　　*block plaid* 大方格
- *tartan plaid* 格子花　　　*printed pattern* 印花
- **stars** 〔stɑrz 〕*n.* 星點花
- *pin check* 細格子　　　　*pin stripes* 細條紋
- **stripes** 〔straɪps 〕*n.* 條紋
- *fancy twill* 斜紋布　　　*hard knot* 死結
- **flounce** 〔flaʊns 〕*n.* 荷葉邊

5 We use the centimeter in Taiwan.
説明尺寸單位及限制

—— ＜會話實況＞——

　　台灣與其他國家**計量的單位**或有不同，故出售貨品給外國人時，必須加以解釋清楚，以免發生誤解。如：*We sell coffee beans by the gram.* 我們賣咖啡豆是按克計算的。以下是一些常用的會話。

Dialogue 1

C : **What do you mean by 25?** 你說25是什麼意思？

S : That's **in centimeters. We use the centimeter in Taiwan.**
　　那是公分單位。台灣用公分爲單位。

Dialogue 2

C : Do you sell coffee beans **by the pound**?
　　你賣咖啡豆是按英磅計算的嗎？

S : No, by the gram. But we can **convert** it right away.
　　不，以公克計算。不過我們可以立刻換算。

Dialogue 3

S : Do you know your size in centimeters?
　　您知道您公分單位的尺寸嗎？

C : No, **I'm not used to it yet.**
　　不，我還不習慣用公分。

Dialogue 4

C : I want 10 feet of this. 這個我要十英呎。

S : I'm sorry, ma'am. *We sell material by the meter.* But we can *convert* it right away... That's about 3 meters, ma'am.
抱歉，女士。我們賣布料是以公尺來計算的。不過我們可以馬上換算⋯⋯。大約是 3 公尺，女士。

C : 3 meters is fine, then. 那就 3 公尺好了。

Dialogue 5

C : Do you have this *in extra-large*?
你們有沒有這種款式特大號的？

S : Yes, but this is the largest we carry at this department. *How would you like to go to our king-size department*?
有的，不過這件是這個部門中所存最大的一件，您要到我們的超大號部門看一下嗎？

Dialogue 6

C : *Is it the largest made*?
這是這家製造商出廠的款式中最大的一件嗎？

S : No, sir. We have some larger ones by this producer, but they are in the king-size department.
不，先生，我們還有一些由這家製造商出廠的較大尺寸的衣服，但是都放在超大號部門中。

Dialogue 7

C : Can I get larger ones if I go to your queen-size department? 我能在你們的超大號部門中找到較大尺寸的嗎？

S : No, ma'am. This size is the largest made by Polo.

不，女士。這種尺寸是 Polo 製造的最大尺寸了。

Dialogue 8

C : Excuse me. I'm looking for an extra-large in this but I can't find any here.

對不起，我想在這裏找一件特大號的，但一直找不到。

S : I'm sorry, but this is *the largest in this style.*

抱歉，但這件是這種款式中最大的一件了。

 # Useful Examples

活用例句

① We *go by* the centimeter in Taiwan.

We use the centimeter (metric system) in Taiwan.

① 在台灣是用十進位制。

② We sell coffee *by the gram.*

② 咖啡按公克售賣。

③ We sell material *by the meter.*

③ 我們售賣布料以公尺計算。

④ Do you know your size *in centimeters*?

④ 您知道您公分單位的尺寸嗎？

⑤ We can *convert* it right away.

⑤ 我們可以馬上換算。

⑥ What do you mean by 'gram'?

⑥ 你說公克是什麼意思？

⑦ I'm not used to that.

⑦ 我對那還不習慣。

⑧ I'm sorry, but this is *the largest size we carry at*（*in*）*this department.*

I'm sorry, but we don't carry anything larger at（in）this department.

⑧ 抱歉，但這是我們存放於此部門中最大的尺寸。

抱歉，但我們在此部門中沒有更大的了。

⑨ *How would you like to go to our king-size department?*

⑨ 你要到我們的超大部門去看一看嗎？

⑩ Size L is the largest here.

⑩ L 尺寸是這裏最大的。

⑪ We have extra-large（larger ones）in blue jeans, but they are at *the king-size*（*queen-size*）*department.*

⑪ 我們有牛仔褲的特大號尺寸（更大的尺寸），但是它們存放於超大部門中。

⑫ This is the largest size in this style.

⑫ 這件是這種款式中最大的尺寸。

⑬ *Is it the largest made*（size）?

⑬ 這是這家製造商所出廠最大的嗎？

⑭ Can I get the size if I got to your king-size department?

⑭ 我能在你們的超大部門找到那種尺寸嗎？

【 註 】━━━━━━━━━━━━◆◆

bean〔bin〕*n.*豆　　pound〔paʊnd〕*n.*磅
gram〔græm〕*n.*克　　convert〔kən'vɝt〕*v.*改變
material〔mə'tɪrɪəl〕*n.*布料；材料　　meter〔'mitɚ〕*n.*公尺
metric system 米突制；十進制　　extra〔'ɛkstrə〕*adj.* 特別地
king-size〔'kɪŋ,saɪz〕*adj.* 特大的

It's made of 100% cotton.
説明材質

──<會話實況>──

　　服飾的流行款式及**質感**是可以和顧客詳盡深刻地說明的題材，
所以此時務必要簡單明瞭地向顧客解釋 *cotton* 棉，*silk* 絲，以及
organdy 麻紗等各種質料的特色與區別，讓顧客有多重選擇的機會。

Dialogue 1

C : ***Which is softer to the touch***? 哪件摸起來較柔軟？

S : This one here, because it's ***made of 100% cotton.***
　　這邊這件，因為它是百分之百純棉製的。

Dialogue 2

S : Which material would you like? We have cotton and polyester.
　　您要哪種質料？我們有棉製的和合成料的。

C : *Whichever one is softer to the touch.*
　　摸起來較柔軟的那種。

S : Then cotton is better. 那麼，棉製的較佳。

Dialogue 3

C : Which one ***absorbs your perspiration*** better?
　　哪件較吸汗？

S : This one here. It's made of 100% cotton.
　　這邊這件。百分之百純棉製的。

這是百分之百純棉製的。

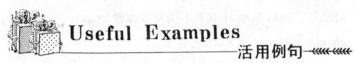

Useful Examples
————————————活用例句————

① **What kind of material** would you like?

　　您要什麼樣的質料？

② This is much softer to the touch because it's **made of 100% cotton.**

　　這摸起來較柔軟，因為是百分之百純棉製的。

③ This has 35% polyester, so I think the other one **absorbs your perspiration better.**

　　這件有百分之三十五的合成纖維，所以我想另一件比較吸汗。

④ **Whichever is softer to the touch.** 摸起來較柔軟的那種。

【註】————————————◆◆

cotton〔'katn̩〕*n.* 棉　　　polyester〔,palɪ'ɛstɚ〕*n.*〔化〕多元脂

whichever〔hwɪtʃ'ɛvɚ〕*pron., adj.* 任何一個；無論何者

absorb〔əb'sɔrb〕*v.* 吸收

perspiration〔,pɝspə'reʃən〕*n.* 汗

衣料專用術語

- **rayon**〔'reɑn〕 *n.* 人造絲
- *indanthrene-blue cloth* 陰丹士林布
- *cotton fabric* 棉織品
- **organdy**〔'ɔrgəndɪ〕 *n.* 蔴紗
- *plain satin* 素緞
- **khaki**〔'kɑkɪ〕 *n.* 卡其布（通常作複數 khakis）
- **chintz**〔tʃɪnts〕 *n.* 印花棉布
- *synthetic leather* 合成皮
- **velvet**〔'vɛlvɪt〕 *n.* 絲絨

- **calfskin**〔'kæf,skɪn〕 *n.* 小牛皮；犢皮
- **mink**〔mɪŋk〕 *n.* 貂皮
- *man-made leather* 人造皮
- **kidskin**〔'kɪd,skɪn〕 *n.* 小山羊皮
- **goatskin**〔'got,skɪn〕 *n.* 山羊皮
- *buffalo hide* 水牛皮　　　　**fur**〔fɝ〕 *n.* 毛皮
- **cowhide**〔'kaʊ,haɪd〕 *n.* 牛皮（＝ leather〔'lɛðɚ〕）
- **mohair**〔'mo,hɛr〕 *n.* 毛海；仿毛衣料
- **wool**〔wʊl〕 *n.* 毛料

7 Which wears better?
說明耐久性

<會話實況>

　　商品的主要價值取決於品質的**耐久性**，因此這類相關話題必須詳細深入的了解，才能清楚地向顧客說明，*This is much more durable.* 這個耐用得多。以下收錄幾則對話可供參考。

Dialogue 1

C: *Which wears better?* 哪個較耐用？

S: I *recommend* this one. It's made of genuine leather. *It's a little expensive, though.*
　　我推薦這個。它是真皮做的。雖然有點貴。

Dialogue 2

S: This will *wear much longer than* this one.
　　這個會比這個耐久的多。

C: Are you sure? 真的？

S: Yes, *absolutely.* 是的，絕對會。

 Useful Examples
───────活用例句─≪≪≪≪≪≪

① *This is much more durable.* 這個耐用得多。

② This *is made of* genuine leather, so it will *wear well.*
　　這是用真皮做的，所以很耐用。

③ *Which wears better?* 哪樣較耐用？

皮革專用術語

- *wear well* 耐久；耐穿
- **genuine** 〔'dʒɛnjʊɪn〕*adj.* 眞正的；非僞造的
- **leather** 〔'lɛðə〕*n.* 皮革
- *genuine leather* 眞皮　　　　*artificial leather* 人造皮
- **durable** 〔'djʊrəbḷ〕*adj.* 耐久的
- **rabbit** 〔'ræbɪt〕*n.* 兔皮（＝ *rabbit fur*）
- *tiger skin* 虎皮
- **fox** 〔fɑks〕*n.* 狐皮
- **worsted** 〔'wʊstɪd〕*n.* 呢料
- **flannel** 〔'flænḷ〕*n.* 法蘭絨
- **leopard** 〔'lɛpəd〕*n.* 豹皮（＝ *leopard skin*）
- *horse hide* 馬皮
- **seal** 〔sil〕*n.* 海豹皮（＝ *seal skin*）
- **beaver** 〔'bivə〕*n.* 海狸皮
- **snakeskin** 〔'snek,skɪn〕*n.* 蛇皮
- **rawhide** 〔'rɔ,haɪd〕*n.* 生皮（＝ pelt〔pɛlt〕）
- **beige** 〔beʒ〕*n.* 本色毛呢
- **hide** 〔haɪd〕*n.* 皮張；生皮（＝ skin〔skɪn〕）
- **alligator** 〔'ælə,getə〕*n.* 鱷魚皮（＝ *alligator skin*）

8 How do you prevent discoloration?
說明洗滌方法

＜會話實況＞

接待外國觀光客和本地顧客時，必須依照其不同的生活、氣候給予其所購買物品**保養的方法**，這是一個好的售貨員最基本的常識。如 *It's better to wash it in cold water.* 最好用冷水清洗。

Dialogue 1

C : What do you suggest so I can *keep it from shrinking*?
　　你說我要怎樣才能防止它縮水？

S : It's better to take it to *a dry cleaner's*.
　　最好交給乾洗店洗。

Dialogue 2

C : How do you *prevent discoloration*?
　　要如何防止褪色？

S : It's better to wash it in cold water.
　　最好在冷水中清洗。

Dialogue 3

C : Can I *machine wash* it? 可以用洗衣機洗嗎？

S : Yes, but it's better to turn it inside out when you wash it, so you can *keep the surface from pilling*.
　　可以，但洗的時候最好把裏面翻出來，這樣可以避免起毛球。

Dialogue 4

C : Can I wash it with other clothes?
　我可以將它和其他衣服一起洗嗎？

S : Yes, but it's better to **button the buttons** when washing
　it, so you can keep it from **going out of shape**.
　可以，但洗的時候最好扣上扣子，這樣可以防止變形。

 # Useful Examples
—————————————————————活用例句→«««‹«««

① It's better to take it to **a dry cleaner's**.

　① 最好送給乾洗店洗。

② It's better to **wash it in cold water**.

　② 最好在冷水中清洗。

③ It's better to wash it **by hand**.

　③ 最好用手洗。

④ It's better to **turn it inside out** when you wash it, so you can **keep** the surface **from pilling**.

　④ 洗的時候最好把裏面翻出來，這樣可以防止起毛球。

⑤ It's better to button the buttons when washing it, so you can keep it from **going out of shape**.

　⑤ 洗的時候最好扣上扣子，這樣可以防止變形。

⑥ It's better to **dry it in the shade**.

　⑥ 最好在陰涼處陰乾。

⑦ **This will never fade.**
　(=*This is fade-proof.*)

　⑦ 永不褪色。

⑧ What do you suggest so I can
  keep it *from shrinking*?

⑨ How do you *prevent discoloration*?

ⓐ 你說要怎樣才能防止它
  縮水？

⑨ 怎樣防止褪色？

shrink〔ʃrɪŋk〕*v., n.* 收縮
cleaner〔'klinɚ〕*n.* 乾洗店
prevent〔prɪ'vɛnt〕*v.* 阻礙；預防
discoloration〔dɪs,kʌlə'reʃən〕*n.* 變色；污染
pill〔pɪl〕*v.* （毛線衣）起毛球
button〔'bʌtn̩〕*v.* 扣（鈕扣）   *n.* 鈕扣
shape〔ʃep〕*n.* 形狀   shade〔ʃed〕*n.* 蔭涼處
fadeproof〔'fed,pruf〕*adj.* 不褪（色）的

This is the largest one we have in stock right now.
説明存貨

┌─**<會話實況>**─────────────────────

售貨期間常常會發生**現貨不足**的情況，尤其西方觀光客體格碩
大，通常沒有適合他們的尺寸，此時則須再訂購或者說抱歉了。
We can order it. Shall we? 我們會再訂購的，好嗎？

└────────────────────────────────────

Dialogue 1

S : *How are you doing, sir?* 先生，怎麼樣？

C : Oh, no. It's too small for me. *It doesn't fit.* Do you have
 a larger one?

  喔，不好。我穿太小了。不合身。有大一點的嗎？

S : I'm really sorry, sir, but this is *the largest one we have
 in stock* right now.

  眞的很抱歉，先生，但這是我們現有存貨中最大的一件。

Dialogue 2

C : That's obviously too small for me. Don't you have a larger
 one?

  很明顯我穿太小了。沒有大一點的嗎？

S : No, we don't have anything larger in stock at the moment.
 I'm sorry. But *we can order it. Shall we?*

  沒有，我們現在的存貨中沒有更大的。很抱歉。不過我們會訂貨。
  好嗎？

Dialogue 3

C : That's all you have here? 那是你們在這裏所有的東西嗎？

S : Yes, but we have some more on the 3rd floor, so *would you like to check it out there*?

　　是的，但我們還有一些在三樓，所以您要去看看嗎？

C : O.K. I will. 好的。我要去。

Dialogue 4

C : I want 10 of them. 我想要十個。

S : I'm sorry, but we only have 6 in stock right now.

　　很抱歉，我們現在只有 6 個存貨。

Dialogue 5

C : Can you give me *another new pair*?

　　你能給我另外一雙新的嗎？

S : I'm sorry, but these are the last ones.... How would you like these, *instead*?

　　抱歉，但這是最後的存貨了，您覺得換另外這種如何？

C : Hmm... Not bad. But *let me think it over*.

　　呣……還不錯。但讓我考慮一下。

Dialogue 6

C : I want the same one as the one *in this catalogue* here.

　　我要像這目錄上一樣的那個。

S : Just a moment, please. I'll go and check it out... I'm sorry, but we don't have that one in stock right now.

　　請等一下，我去找找看……抱歉，我們現在沒有那種的存貨。

Dialogue 7

C : I want a blue one *with the same design.*

我要一個藍色的，跟這種相同款式的。

S : I'm sorry, but this is the last one.

抱歉，但這是最後一個了。

Dialogue 8

C : I want a red one *in the same size.*

我要一個紅色的，這種尺寸的。

S : I'm sorry, but this is all we have right now.

抱歉，我們現在僅有這種的。

Dialogue 9

C : Do you have this? (*She holds out a description.*)

你們有這個嗎？（她拿出一份說明書。）

S : Yes, we do. Just a moment, please... I'm sorry, but they are *out of stock* at the moment.

有的，請稍等……很抱歉，現在缺貨。

Useful Examples

活用例句 ►◄◄◄◄◄◄◄

① I'm sorry, but this is *the largest* (*smallest*) *one we have* in stock at the moment.
I'm sorry, but we don't have *anything larger* (*smaller*) in stock right now.

① 抱歉，但這是目前存貨中最大（小）的一件了。

② We have some more on the 7th floor.

② 我們在七樓還有一些。

③ Would you like to *check* it *out* there?

③ 你要去那裏看看嗎？

④ *It doesn't fit.*

④ 不合身。

⑤ I'm sorry, but it (this/that) is *the last one.*
I'm sorry, but they (these/those) are *the last ones.*
I'm sorry, but this (that) is *all we have in stock* right now.

⑤ 抱歉，它（這／那）是最後一個。
抱歉，它們（這些／那些）是最後的存貨。
抱歉，這（那）是我們現在僅有的存貨。

⑥ I'm sorry, but *it's* (*they are*) *out of stock.*
I'm sorry, but we *don't have any* in stock.

⑥ 抱歉，現在缺貨。
抱歉，我們沒有任何存貨。

⑦ I'm sorry, but we only have two *left*.

⑦ 很抱歉，我們祇剩二個。

⑧ How would you like this one (these), *instead*?

⑧ 您覺得改用這個（些）代替如何？

⑨ Can you give me another new pair?

⑨ 你能給我另一雙新的嗎？

⑩ I want a blue one *with* (=*in*) *the same design*.

I want a red one *in the same size*.

⑩ 我要一個跟這相同款式，藍色的。

我要一個紅色的，跟這相同尺寸的。

⑪ I want *the same one as the one in the catalogue* here.

⑪ 我要和這目錄上相同的這一種。

---

obviously〔'ɑbvɪəslɪ〕*adv*. 顯然地

order〔'ɔrdɚ〕*v.*, *n.* 訂貨

floor〔flɔr〕*n.* 樓層

pair〔pɛr；pær〕*n.* 一組；一對

think over 仔細考慮

catalogue〔'kætḷ,ɔg〕*n.* 目錄；貨物價目表

description〔dɪ'skrɪpʃən〕*n.* 說明；描寫

10 It's not for sale.
説明非賣品及成套出售

┌─ <會話實況> ─
│   百貨商店常常發生顧客看上**非賣品**或者**成套**產品中的一個的情
│ 事，此時拒絕購買又很難開口，因此必須對其解釋淸楚不能賣的理
│ 由，例如：*It's part of the decoration.* 它是裝飾的一部份。
└

Dialogue 1

C : How much is this? 這個多少錢？

S : I'm sorry, but *it's not for sale.* It's *part of the decoration.* 抱歉，它是非賣品。祇是裝飾的一部分。

C : Really? *Where can I get it*? 眞的嗎？我在哪裏可以買到呢？

S : I don't think you can get it in Taiwan. 我想在台灣買不到。

C : Oh, okay. 噢，好吧。

Dialogue 2

C : I want *the same* one *as* this one. 我要一個和這個一樣的。

S : I'm sorry, but they are *for export*, and not for sale in Taiwan. 對不起，他們專供外銷，在台灣是非賣品。

Dialogue 3

C : Are you selling this? 你賣這個嗎？

S : No, sir. *It's just for display.* 不。它祇是展覽品。

C : Oh, I see. 噢，我明白了。

Dialogue 4

C : Isn't it too expensive? 不嫌太貴了嗎?

S : That's *the price for the whole set*, ma'am.
夫人，那是一整組的價格。

Dialogue 5

C : *How much is it per piece*? 每件多少錢?

S : I'm sorry, but we don't sell them *separately*.
抱歉，我們不分開賣的。

 # Useful Examples
活用例句

① I'm sorry, *but it's not for sale.*　　　①對不起，它是非賣品。

② I'm sorry, but *they're not for sale* in Taiwan.
I'm sorry, but *they're not sold* in Taiwan.
I'm sorry, but they *cannot be purchased* in Taiwan.

②抱歉，在台灣它們是非賣品。
對不起，在台灣它們不出售。
抱歉，在台灣它們不可能被買到。

③ *It is* (*they are*) *for export.*　　　③它(們)是外銷品。

④ It is (they are) *for display* (, only).
④它(們)(祇)是用來展覽的。

⑤ It is (they are) *part of the decoration.*
⑤它(們)是裝飾的一部分。

⑥ This is the price for ***the whole set***.

⑥ 這是一整組的價格。

⑦ I'm sorry, but we don't ***sell them separately*** (individually).

⑥ 抱歉，我們不分開（個別）賣的。

⑧ How much is it ***per piece***?

⑧ 這一件賣多少？

for sale 出售（= *on sale*）
decoration〔,dɛkə'reʃən〕*n.* 裝飾品
export〔ıks'port〕*v.* 外銷　〔'ɛksport〕*n.*
display〔dı'sple〕*n.,v.* 陳列；展覽
set〔sɛt〕*n.* 套；組
per〔pɚ〕*prep.* 每

11 Shall we order some more?
説明訂購事宜及所需時間

<會話實況>

　　有關產品庫存的情形是售貨員務必要學習的一課，其中最基本的是要區別 *order* **訂購**，和 *on order* **訂購中**的意思。因為物品的訂購事宜已經十分風行，顧客逛街已經不再像從前那樣提著大筆現金去逛街購物，或大包小包辛苦地提回家。

Dialogue 1

C : I want this size in *the same* design *as* that one.

　　我要這個尺寸，而式樣和那個相同的。

S : I'm sorry, this is all we have, but *I think it can be ordered.* I'll go and check with the producer.

　　很抱歉，這是我們全部所有的，但我想可以再訂貨。我會去向製造商查詢一下。

Dialogue 2

C : I bought 10 of these china plates here last week, but *they are not enough.*

　　上星期我在這裏買了十個瓷盤，但還嫌不夠。

S : Oh, I see. Just a moment, please.... We only have 2 left, so *shall we order some more*?

　　喔，我明白了。請稍等一下……我們祇剩二個，要不要再訂購一些？

Dialogue 3

C : Don't you have a black one in the same design?
你們沒有相同式樣黑色的嗎?

S : Not at this moment. *They're really popular, so they sell very fast.* But they are *on order*, so we'll have one soon. I'll go and ask the producer *how much longer it will take.*
現在沒有。他們真的很暢銷,所以很快就賣完了。但我們已經訂購了一批,應該很快就會送到。我去問問看製造商還要多久。

Dialogue 4

C : How long do I have to wait? 我必須等多久?
S : *It will take a few days.* 要幾天。

Dialogue 5

C : When should I come back? 我什麼時候回來拿?
S : We expect to *have it back* the day after tomorrow.
我們預計後天應該會好。

Dialogue 6

C : How much longer will it take? 還要花多久時間?
S : I think it will take *another couple of* days.
我想還需要好幾天。
C : Oh, no. I can't wait that long. Why so long?
喔,不行,我不能等那麼久。為什麼要那麼久呢?
S : *We're in the busy period.* I'm sorry, but there's nothing we can do about it.
我們這段時間是旺季。很抱歉,實在是沒辦法。

Useful Examples
活用例句

① *It* (*they*) *can be ordered.* ① 它可以用訂購的。

② *Shall we order it* (them)? ② 我們要訂購嗎？

③ Shall we order some more? ③ 我們要不要多訂一點？

④ It's (they are) *on order* at the moment. ④ 現在它（們）已訂購了。

⑤ I'll go and *check with* the producer.
   ask the producer.
   inquire of the producer.
⑤ 我會和製造商查詢一下。
   問一問製造商。
   詢問一下製造商。

⑥ We'll get it (them) for you by next Monday. ⑥ 下週一之前我們會把它（們）寄給您。

⑦ They are not enough. ⑦ 他們還不夠。

⑧ I think *it will take a few* (*about 2 or 3*) *days.* ⑧ 我想要花上幾（大約2、3）天的時間。

⑨ It will take another 4 or 5 days. ⑨ 還要再4、5天的時間。

⑩ *It will be ready by* then. ⑩ 在那時候會準備好。

⑪ *We expect to have it back* in two days. ⑪ 我們預計兩天內會好。

【註】

inquire of 詢問　　*couple of days* 數天

交易專用術語

- **producer**〔prə'djusɚ〕*n*. 製造商；生產者
- *pay in one lump sum* 一次總付
- (*deal*) *cannot be closed* 不能成交
- *completion of business transaction* 銀貨兩訖
  (= *goods received and payment made*)
- *down payment* 定金
- **deposit**〔dɪ'pɑzɪt〕*n*. 押金；存款；保證金
- *item number* 物品編號
- *uniform invoice* 統一發票

- *black market price* 黑市價
- **contract**〔'kɑntrækt〕*n*. 契據（簽名蓋章）
- *all sales are final* 恕不退換
- *credit card* 信用卡
- *charge account* 賒帳
- *telephone order* 電話購買(= *purchase by phone*)
- *futures market* 期貨市場
- *cash market* 現貨市場
- appraisal〔ə'prezḷ〕*n*. 估價單

12 We have a manual written in English.
說明書及保證

──＜會話實況＞──

　　有些商品因新穎或者看來陌生，都需要**說明書**來詳述使用方法，因此面對外國顧客，最好先告知附有英文說明書，*We have a manual written in English.* 我們有英文說明書。以節省複雜的解釋時間。

Dialogue 1

C : Do you have *a manual written in English*?
　　你們有沒有英文手册？

S : Yes, we do... Here you are.
　　有的，我們有……在這裏。

C : How much is it? 多少錢？

S : Oh, no. *You don't need to pay for this.*（*It's free.*）
　　喔，不用。你不需要付錢。（免費的。）

Dialogue 2

C : *How do I use it*?
　　我要怎麼使用呢？

S : *The instructions* are given here in English.
　　英文的說明書在這裏。

C : Oh, thank you. 喔，謝謝。

我們有英文說明書。

WE HAVE A MANUAL WRITTEN IN ENGLISH.

Dialogue 3

C : *Is it under warranty* for some period?
有保證有效期間嗎？

S : Yes, sir. For one year.... This is your *warranty certificate.*
有的，先生。一年……這是您的保證書。

C : Oh, thank you. 喔，謝謝。

Dialogue 4

S : *The warranty is only good for 6 months.* So please remember that.
保證期間只有六個月。請記得。

C : O.K., but why only 6 months?
好的，但是為什麼只有六個月？

S : I have no idea, but this is *what the producer says.*
我不知道，但是這是製造廠商說的。

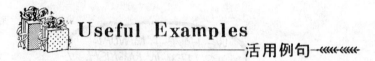

Useful Examples
活用例句

① We have *a manual written in English.*

我們有英文手冊。

② *The instructions* are given here *in English.*

英文的說明書在這裏。

③ This will show you how to use it.

這個會指示您使用的方法。

④ Do you have an English manual?

你們有英文手冊嗎？

⑤ Do you have a manual written in English?

你們有沒有英文手冊呢？

⑥ This is your *warranty certificate.*

這是您的保證書。

⑦ The warranty is only good for 6 months.

保證期間只有六個月。

⑧ The warranty will *expire* after 6 months.

保證六個月後期滿。

【註】

manual〔'mænjuəl〕*n.* 手冊

free〔fri〕*adj.* 免費的；自由的

warranty〔'wɔrəntɪ〕*n.* 保證；擔保契約

certificate〔sə'tɪfəkɪt〕*n.* 證書

expire〔ɪk'spaɪr〕*v.* 期滿；終止

13

Would you like to have it delivered?

運送須知(費用、日期等)

<會話實況>

顧客有時會因携帶不便或物品太多太重而希望商品代為**運送**，有此種售後服務的商店店員則必須主動說：*Would you like to have it delivered?* 您要我們代為運送嗎？然後說明費用（charge）及日期（date）。以下例舉幾種能讓您隨機應變的對話。

Dialogue 1

S : Would you like to *take it with* you or *have it delivered*?
　　您想自己帶走還是經由遞送？
C : I want it delivered. 我要經由遞送。
S : Then, *may I have your name, address, and telephone number on this slip*?
　　那麼，請將您的大名、住址及電話填在這張紙上好嗎？

Dialogue 2

C : *When will it reach me*? 什麼時候送到？
S : You will probably get it in about 4 days.
　　您大概會在四天左右收到。

Dialogue 3

C : How much does it cost *for delivery*? 運費要多少？
S : It's *free of charge* within the Taipei area, sir.
　　在台北市區內免費，先生。

Dialogue 4

C : Is it free *all over* the country? 全國都免費嗎？

S : No, ma'am. Only within the Taipei metropolitan area. Outside this area, it's $1,500. 不是的，女士。只有在大台北地區內免費。台北以外的地區要 1500 元。

C : O.K. Then I'll take it home with me.
好吧！那我要自己帶回家。

Dialogue 5

C : *How much does it cost extra* if you put it in a box?
如果裝箱要多付多少錢？

S : $50 ma'am. Is that all right? 50 元，女士。那樣可以嗎？

C : O.K. 好的。

Dialogue 6

S : Where is it, sir? 在哪裏，先生？

C : Keelung. 基隆。

S : Delivery is charged outside the Taipei metropolitan area. Is that all right?
大台北地區以外運送要收費的。可以嗎？

C : It doesn't *include my neighborhood*?
不包括我的鄰近地區嗎？

S : No, sir. 不，先生。

C : All right. How much is it?
好吧。多少錢？

S : $450 for Keelung. 到基隆 450 元。

C : O.K. 好的。

Dialogue 7

S : Would you like to *specify a date*? 您要指定日期嗎？

C : Oh, I can do that? 喔，可以嗎？

S : Certainly. 當然可以。

Dialogue 8

S : What day would suit you? 哪一天您覺得合適？

C : I work from Monday through Saturday, so Sunday *is best for me*.

　　我星期一到星期六都上班，所以星期天最適合我。

S : Then, would next Sunday be all right? 那麼，下星期天好嗎？

C : *No problem*. 沒問題。

Dialogue 9

C : Can I specify a date? 我可以指定日期嗎？

S : Yes, but *the earliest date possible* is the 18th.

　　可以，但是最早可能是十八號。

Dialogue 10

C : I want it in the morning. 我要早上送到。

S : I'm sorry, but you can't specify the time.

　　抱歉，但是您不可以指定時間。

C : Even morning or afternoon? 連早上或下午都不可以指定嗎？

S : No, sir. 不可以的，先生。

C : O.K., then *what's the earliest time they might come*?

　　好吧，那他們最早可能幾點來？

S : Around 10:00. 大約十點。

Useful Examples

活用例句

① *Would you like to take it with you or have it delivered*?

② Then, *may I have your name, address, and telephone number on this slip*? (Would you please *fill out* this slip?)

③ I think you will probably get it in 3 days.

④ It will take about 3 days.

⑤ *I want it delivered.*

⑥ When will it reach me?

⑦ Delivery is *free of charge* (within the Taipei metropolitan area).
We don't charge for delivery (within the Taipei area).

⑧ *Delivery is charged* outside Taipei.
We charge for delivery outside Taipei.

⑨ Is it free all over the country?

① 您想親自帶走還是經由遞送?

② 那麼,可以將您的大名、住址及電話填在這張紙上嗎?(請填好這張表格好嗎?)

③ 我想您可能在三天後收到。

④ 大約要花三天。

⑤ 我要它送過來。

⑥ 什麼時候送到?

⑦ 運送(在大台北地區內)免費。

(在台北市區內)我們不收運費。

⑧ 台北市區以外運貨要收費。
我們運貨到台北以外的地區要收費。

⑨ 全國都免費嗎?

⑩ A box costs $50. Is that all right?

⑩ 一個箱子50元，可以嗎？

⑪ *How much does it cost extra* if I specify a date?

⑪ 如果我指定日期要多付多少錢？

⑫ It costs NT$50 extra.

⑫ 要額外花50元。

⑬ It costs another NT$50.

⑬ 要多花50元。

⑭ *Would you like to specify a date*?

⑭ 您要指定日期嗎？

⑮ *What day would suit you*?

⑮ 哪一天適合您？

⑯ What day (time) would be convenient for you?

⑯ 您哪一天較方便？

⑰ *The earliest date possible is* Friday.

⑰ 最早的一天可能是星期五。

⑱ Delivery is not *available*.

⑱ 不送貨。

⑲ I'm sorry, but you can't *specify the time*.

⑲ 抱歉，但是您不可以指定時間。

⑳ Even morning or afternoon?

⑳ 甚至早上或者下午？

【註】────────────◆◆

slip 〔 slɪp 〕 *n.* 紙條；單子   *fill out* 填好
metropolitan 〔 ,mɛtrə'pɑlətṇ 〕 *n.* 大都市
neighborhood 〔 'nebɚ,hʊd 〕 *n.* 鄰近地區
specify 〔 'spɛsə,faɪ 〕 *v.* 指定
available 〔 ə'veləbḷ 〕 *adj.* 可用的

14 Shall I gift-wrap it?
包裝説明一

<會話實況>

當客人要求**包裝**禮品時，當然要以 *certainly*. 好的。來接受，但一般售貨員最好主動詢問顧客有關包裝的需要，才算服務周到。

Dialogue 1

S : Would you like this **gift-wrapped**? 您要包裝這件禮品嗎？

C : Please, and **could you use red wrapping paper**?
好的，可以用紅色的包裝紙嗎？

S : Sure. 當然可以。

Dialogue 2

S : Shall I gift-wrap it for you, madam?
女士，您要我爲您包裝嗎？

C : No, I like to **do it myself**. Do you sell **wrapping paper**?
不要，我要自己包裝。你們有沒有賣包裝紙？

S : No, I'm sorry we don't. 沒有，很抱歉。

 Useful Examples
活用例句

① **Shall I gift-wrap it, sir (ma'am)?**

① 先生（女士），要我把它包裝起來嗎？

② Please wrap it as a gift.

② 請將它包裝成禮品。

③ *How do you want it wrapped*?

③ 您要什麼樣子的包裝？

④ *Would this be all right*?

④ 這樣好嗎？

⑤ Shall I put it in a box?

⑤ 要我把它放進盒子裏嗎？

⑥ There is *a charge for the box*. Will it be all right?

⑥ 盒子要加收費用的，可以嗎？

⑦ I have put *identifying marks* on them.

⑦ 我在它們上面加了識別標籤。

⑧ Would you like to *use our card*?

⑧ 您想用我們店裏的卡片嗎？

⑨ We *normally* use this paper on gifts, so *will it be all right for you too*?

⑨ 我們通常都用這種紙包裝的，您覺得怎樣？

⑩ What does it say?

⑩ 上面寫什麼？

⑪ Shall I *put on* (*write*) your name?

⑪ 要我寫上您的名字嗎？

⑫ Would you like to write your name here?

⑫ 您要在這裏寫上名字嗎？

⑬ Shall we *tie it with a ribbon*?

⑬ 要不要繫上一條緞帶呢？

⑭ What color do you *prefer*?

⑭ 您喜歡什麼顏色？

⑮ We have red, blue and pink ribbons.

⑮ 我們有紅色、藍色和粉紅色的緞帶。

⑯ *Would* a red ribbon *be all right*? ⑯ 紅色緞帶好不好呢？

⑰ We only have a pink ribbon now. ⑰ 我們目前只有粉紅色的
Will it be all right? 緞帶。可以嗎？

【註】━━━━━━━━◆◆

wrap〔ræp〕v. 包裝 *n.* 包裝用料 charge〔tʃɑrdʒ〕v.,n. 索價

identify〔aɪ'dɛntə,faɪ〕v. 認明；鑑定

mark〔mɑrk〕*n.* 記號；標籤 card〔kɑrd〕*n.* 卡片；名片

《 禮物專用術語 》

· 新年祝賀 the new year's greeting

· 新年禮物 a new year's gift

· 中元節禮品 a summer gift

· 年終禮物 a year-end gift

· 謝　禮 a thank you gift

· 離別禮物 a parting (farewell) gift

· 奠　儀 a gift offering to our departed (ones)

＊present 可代替 gift 來使用。

Would you mind changing your money into NT dollars?

15 請求滙兌——

──<會話實況>──

　　與外國客戶交易，不可避免最實際的問題就是**滙兌情事**。各國幣值不同，但最基本要知道外幣交易的技術用語，多用 *exchange* 一字，如 "*foreign exchange*" 外滙，"*exchange rate*" 滙率。

Dialogue 1

C : How much is it *in dollars*? 要美金多少元？

S : Just a moment, please... It's $25.30.
　　請稍候……要 25.30 美元。

C : Then, *here you go.* 那麼，在這裏。

S : I'm sorry, but *we can't accept dollars.*
　　抱歉，但是我們不收美元。

Dialogue 2

C : Do you take dollars? 你們收不收美金？

S : No, sir. I'm sorry. *Would you please change your money into NT dollars*, first?
　　不收，先生。抱歉。請先將您的錢兌換成新台幣好嗎？

Dialogue 3

S : Would you please change your money into NT dollars?
　　請將您的錢換成新台幣好嗎？

C : Where? 在哪裏換？

S : *The money exchange* is on the first floor, at the main entrance. 換錢在一樓，大門處。

Dialogue 4

C : Can I change my money into NT dollars in the store?
我可以在這家店把錢換成新台幣嗎？

S : Yes. *We can take care of it on the first floor at the customer service desk.*
可以，我們在一樓顧客服務台經辦此事。

 Useful Examples
─────────────────────活用例句─《《《《·《《《《

① I'm sorry, but we can't accept dollars（checks）here.
I'm sorry, but you can't use dollars（checks）here.

① 抱歉，但是我們不收美元（支票）。
抱歉，但是您在此不可以用美元（支票）。

② *Would you please change* your money *into* NT dollars?
Would you mind changing your money *into* NT dollars?

② 請將您的錢換成新台幣好嗎？
你介意將你的錢換成新台幣嗎？

③ We can *take care of* the exchange （The money exchange is）on the first floor *at the main entrance.*

③ 我們在一樓大門處經辦兌錢之事。

④ How much is it *in dollars*?

④ 要美金多少元？

⑤ Do you take dollars?

⑤ 你們收不收美金?

⑥ **Will you change it into NT, please**?

⑥ 請您將錢換成台幣好嗎?

⑦ **May we see your passport, please**?

⑦ 我能看看您的護照嗎?

⑧ Will you show us your passport, please?

⑧ 請讓我們看一下您的護照,可以嗎?

⑨ Will you **fill in the blanks**, please?

⑨ 請您填寫空白處好嗎?

accept〔əkˈsɛpt〕*v.* 接受;同意
exchange〔ɪksˈtʃendʒ〕*n.,v.* 滙兌;交易
entrance〔ˈɛntrəns〕*n.* 大門;入口
take care of 處理;經辦
customer〔ˈkʌstəmə〕*n.* 顧客
service〔ˈsɝvɪs〕*n.,v.* 服務
blank〔blæŋk〕*n.* 空白處

滙兌地點術語

- 中央銀行　*Central Bank of China*
- 中國國際商業銀行　*International Commercial Bank of China*
- 中國農民銀行　*Farmer's Bank of China*
- 世界開發銀行　*International Bank for Reconstruction & Development*
- 世華聯合商業銀行　*United World-Chinese Commercial Bank*
- 交通銀行　*Bank of Communications*
- 亞洲開發銀行　*Asian Development Bank*
- 美國大陸銀行臺北分行　*Continental Bank, Taipei Branch*
- 美國太平洋銀行臺北分行　*International Pacific Security Bank, Taipei Branch*
- 美國花旗銀行臺北分行　*City Bank, NA, Taipei Branch*
- 日商第一勸業銀行臺灣分行　*Dai-Ichi Kangyo Bank, Taiwan Branch*
- 美國大通銀行臺北分行　*Chase Manhattan Bank, Taipei Branch*

Exchange Terms

- 美國運通銀行臺北分行　*American Express, Taipei Branch*
- 第一商業銀行　*First Commercial Bank*
- 華南商業銀行　*Hua Nan Commercial Bank*
- 華僑商業銀行　*Overseas Chinese Commercial Banking Corporation*
- 郵政儲金滙業局　*Directorate-General of Postal Remittances & Savings Banks*
- 彰化商業銀行　*Chang Hua Commercial Bank*
- 臺北市第十信用合作社　*The 10th Credit Cooperative of Taipei*
- 臺北市銀行　*City Bank of Taipei*
- 臺灣土地銀行　*Land Bank of Taiwan*
- 臺灣中小企業銀行　*Medium Business Bank of Taiwan*
- 臺灣省合作金庫　*Co-operative Bank of Taiwan*
- 臺灣銀行　*Bank of Taiwan*
- 國際決算銀行　*Bank for International Settlement*
- 美國商業銀行臺北分行　*Bank of America, Taipei Branch*

16 We have a cash-on-delivery system.
定金及餘款的説明

＜會話實況＞

交易買賣時，如果買賣雙方都有足夠的信用度，則通常會有先付**定金**的情形，而現今很流行一種**貨到付現**的服務，*cash on delivery* 就是貨物送到家後，買方再付現款的情形，十分方便。

Dialogue 1

C： Do I have to pay now? 我現在就必須付錢嗎？

S： No, ma'am. You can pay us *when it's ready.* But would you please *deposit some money with us*? 不用的，女士。您方便時再付給我們。但您可不可以先交給我們一些保證金？

C： How much? 多少？

S： $1,000 is enough. 一千元就夠了。

C： Sure. 好的。

Dialogue 2

C： How long will it take? 要多久時間？

S： About 2 weeks. 大約兩星期。

C： That long? 那麼久啊？

S： Yes, I'm sorry, but it always takes about 2 weeks. *Would you please pay for your purchase now*?

是的，抱歉，但是通常都要兩星期。請您現在付款好嗎？

C： All right. 好吧。

Dialogue 3

C : I don't have cash today. 我今天沒帶現金。

S : That's okay. We have *a cash-on-delivery system*, so you can
make your payment at home (on delivery).

　　沒關係。我們有貨到才付款的制度，所以您可以在家收了貨再付
現金。

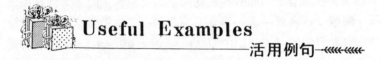

Useful Examples
————————————————————活用例句→«««-««««

① You can pay us *when it is ready*.

　　您可以方便時再付款給我們。

② Would you please *pay for your purchase* now?

　　請您現在付款好嗎？

③ *We have a cash-on-delivery system*.

　　我們有貨到付現的制度。

④ Would you please *deposit* some money *with* us?

　　請先交一些保證金給我們好嗎？

　　Would you please *make a down payment*?

　　請先付定金好嗎？

⑤ May we have *a deposit*? 請您先交保證金好嗎？

⑥ *Cash on delivery* will be all right, sir (ma'am).

　　先生（女士），可以貨到了再付清現款。

【註】————————————◆◆

deposit〔dɪ'pɑzɪt〕*v*. 抵押；交保證金　　purchase〔'pɝtʃəs〕*n*.,*v*. 購買
cash〔kæʃ〕*n*. 現金　　*cash on delivery*(C.O.D) 貨到付款
system〔'sɪstəm〕*n*. 系統；制度　　*down payment* 付定金；頭款

77

They are all on sale.
大拍賣時

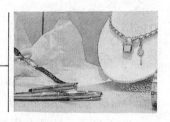

─< 會話實況 >─

　　百貨業者常有季節性的拍賣期間，因此顧客上門通常都會要求**打折**，**降價**，或者買**一送一**等，下面收錄一些常用會話及拍賣術語，讓您置身拍賣場的漫天喊價中，*They are all on sale.* 這些都是要出售的，仍能清楚顧客的喜好，賓主盡歡。

Dialogue 1

C : Are they *cheaper than usual*? 它們比平常便宜嗎？

S : Yes, we are offering them *at half price*.
　　　是的，我們打五折。

C : I see. 我知道了。

Dialogue 2

S : They have a *special* price. 這些是特價。

C : Why so cheap? 爲什麼這麼便宜？

S : Because *we're clearing out our stock* right now.
　　　因爲我們現在正在清倉。

Dialogue 3

C : It's not a mistake? 沒錯嗎？

S : No, ma'am. They are all *on sale*.
　　　沒有錯，女士。這些東西全要出售。

Dialogue 4

C : Can't you make it any cheaper?

不能再便宜一點嗎？

S : I'm sorry, but this is *the best price*. You can't get it any cheaper than here.

抱歉，但是這是最低的價錢了。你買不到比這裏更便宜的了。

C : Are you sure? 你確定嗎？

S : Yes, I'm sure. 確定。

Dialogue 5

S : *I think it's a good purchase to make.*

我認爲這是公道的。

C : Why? 爲什麼？

S : Well, it's really *inexpensive for the quality.*

嗯，就品質而言，它眞的不貴。

Useful Examples

活用例句

① They are *on sale*. 這些物品特價中。（特價中）

They are bargain-priced. 廉價中。

② They have a *special* price. 這些物品正特價中。

③ They have a *reduced* price. 這些物品在減價中。

④ *We are offering them at half price.*

我們以半價提供這些物品。

⑤ I think *it's a good purchase to make.*

我認爲價錢很公道。

⑥ It's *a real bargain.* 這是一樁好買賣。

⑦ You can't get it any cheaper than here.
你買不到比這裏更便宜的了。

⑧ This is *the best quality you can expect.*
這是你能期望最好的品質。

⑨ *Are they cheaper than usual?* 比平常便宜嗎？

⑩ Why so cheap? 爲什麼這麼便宜？

⑪ Can't you make it any cheaper?
不能再便宜一點嗎？

⑫ This is a special price (discount). 這是特價。

⑬ We have a discount of twenty percent.
我們打八折。

⑭ We are *clearing out our stock.* 我們正在清倉特賣。

⑮ This is a special so you can't *return* it.
(= *This is a special so you can't exchange it.*)
這是特價，所以您不能退貨。

---

cheap〔tʃip〕*adj.* 便宜的　　usual〔'juʒʊəl〕*adj.* 通常的
as usual 像平常一樣　　offer〔'ɑfə〕*v., n.* 提供
price〔praɪs〕*n., v.* 價格
special〔'spɛʃəl〕*adj.* 特別的　　*on sale* 出售
inexpensive〔,ɪnɪk'spɛnsɪv〕*adj.* 價廉的
bargain〔'bɑrgɪn〕*n.* 廉售；交易
reduced〔rɪ'djust〕*adj.* 減少的

拍賣專用術語

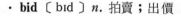

- **bid** 〔 bɪd 〕 *n.* 拍賣；出價　　*successful bidder* 拍賣成交
- **layman** 〔ˈlemən〕 *n.* 外行　　**adept** 〔ˈædɛpt〕 *n.* 內行
- *inside depester* 熟悉內情者
- *introductory goods* 新到貨
- *imitation brand* 冒牌　　*retail market* 零售市場
- **retailer** 〔rɪˈtelɚ〕 *n.* 零售商
- **sale** 〔 sel 〕 *n.* 銷售；拍賣　　*bargain sale* 大廉售
- *bulk sale* 大宗銷售　　*cash sale* 現金銷售
- *commission sale* 寄售　　*compulsory sale* 強迫出售
- *credit sale* 賒售　　*future sale* 期售
- *gross sale* 銷售總額　　*public sale* 公開銷售
- **sample** 〔ˈsæmpḷ〕 *n.* 樣品　　*reserve price* 最低價
- **saleable** 〔ˈseləbḷ〕 *adj.* 暢銷的；易賣的
- **surplus** 〔ˈsɝplʌs〕 *n.* 盈餘；剩餘
- **sight** 〔 saɪt 〕 *n.* 一覽（見）　　**spot** 〔 spɑt 〕 *n.* 現貨；待裝
- *original sample* 原樣品　　*inferior sample* 次級樣品
- **quote** 〔 kwot 〕 *v.* 報價　　**quality** 〔ˈkwɑlətɪ〕 *n.* 品質
- *fair average quality* 中等品
- *quality control* 品管　　*quality guarantee* 品質保證
- **offer** 〔ˈɔfɚ〕 *n., v.* 出價；提供
- *free offer* 自由出價　　*purchase power* 購買力

18 We can't give you any discount.
拒絕減價、小費

<會話實況>

　　接待國外客人時，有一點必須特別注意的就是各個國家之間習慣、風氣等的不同，通常歐美國家的人士有付**小費**的習慣，而東南亞一帶的顧客則喜歡**討價還價**，*Can't you make it cheaper?* 你不能算便宜一點嗎？因此店員必須斟酌情形才能應付裕如。

Dialogue 1

C : Can't you make it cheaper? 不能算便宜一點嗎？

S : I'm sorry, but we can't give you any *discount*.
　　很抱歉，我們不能打折。

C : Why not? 爲什麼？

S : Because *it's our store regulation*. 因爲這是我們店裏的規定。

Dialogue 2

C : Can you give me a discount? 能打折嗎？

S : No, we can't *make any reductions*.
　　不能，我們不打任何折扣。

Dialogue 3

C : *Keep the change*. 零錢不用找了。

S : *It's very kind of you*, but we don't take *tips*. It's our *store rule*. Thank you anyway. 您眞好，但是我們不收小費。
　　這是我們店裏的原則，不過還是謝謝您。

Useful Examples
―――――――――――活用例句―≪≪≪≪≪≪

① I'm sorry, but *we can't make any reductions.* It's our *store rule (policy).*

很抱歉，我們不打任何折扣。這是我們店裏的原則。

② I'm sorry, but we can't *give you any discount.* It's our *store regulation.*

很抱歉，我們不能給您打折。這是我們店裏的規定。

③ It's very kind of you, but *we don't take tips.* Thank you anyway.

您真慷慨，但我們不收小費。無論如何還是謝謝您。

④ Why not? 爲什麼不能？

⑤ *Keep the change.* 不用找了。

⑥ I'm sorry to have kept you waiting. 抱歉讓您久等。

⑦ Thank you. *Please come again.* 謝謝。請再度光臨。

⑧ Thank you for your kindness. 謝謝您的好心。

(= *I am much obliged to you.*)

⑨ I'm sorry. 很抱歉。

⑩ Thank you, but *we can't take tips.*

真謝謝您，我們不收小費。

【註】―――――――――――◆◆

discount〔'dɪskaʊnt〕*n.* 折扣 〔dɪs'kaʊnt〕*v.* 打折
regulation〔,rɛgjə'leʃən〕*n.* 規定
reduction〔rɪ'dʌkʃən〕*n.* 減價   tip〔tɪp〕*n.* 小費
rule〔rul〕*n.* 規則   policy〔'pɑləsɪ〕*n.* 方針；政策

19

Our best offer is 10% off.
說明折扣限度

Dialogue 1

C : I want (to get) it *as* cheap *as possible*.
　　我希望以最低的價錢買到它。

S : Well, *our best offer for today is 25% off.*
　　我們今天的最低價是打七五折。

Dialogue 2

C : Can I get it cheaper *if I pay in cash*?
　　如果我付現金，能算便宜一點嗎？

S : Yes, we can *give you 30% off for cash.*
　　能，現金付款，我們七折優待。

Dialogue 3

C : Can't you *take* a little more *off*?
　　不能再減一點嗎？

S： I'm sorry, that's the best price. We can't sell it any
　　cheaper than that.

　　很抱歉，那是最低的價錢了。我們不能再賣比那更便宜的價錢。

 # Useful Examples
——————————————活用例句→《《《《《《

① *Our best offer* is 10% off.

　　我們最高的限度是打九折。

　　We can't give you more than 10% off.

　　我們無法給你低於九折的折扣。

② *We can give you 15% off for cash.*

　　　現金付款，我們八五折優待。

③ $800 is *the best price*. We can't sell it any cheaper
　　than that.

　　　八百元是最低價。我們無法再賣得更便宜了。

④ I want (to get) it *as cheap as possible*.

　　　我想以最低價買到它。

⑤ Can't you *take a little more off*?

　　　你不能再算便宜點嗎？

【註】————————————————◆◆

off〔ɔf；ɑf〕*n.* 少於；低於

折扣專用術語

- *grand sale* 大廉價
- **lagniappe** 〔læn'jæp〕 *n.* 大贈品
- *bargain price* 討價還價　　*net price* 實價
- *Only one price* 不二價　　*Reduced price* 減價
- *Half price* 半價　　*Special price* 特價
- **discount** 〔'dɪskaʊnt〕 *n.* 折扣
- *trade discount* 同行折扣　　*extra discount* 額外折扣
- *5% off* 九五折
- **rebate** 〔rɪ'bet〕 *n.* 部分回扣

- *rebate coupon* 優待券　　*gift coupon* 禮券
- *blind competition* 惡性競爭
- *office copy* 存根
- **exotic** 〔ɪg'zɑtɪk〕 *n.* 舶來品
- **patent** 〔'pætn̩t〕 *n.* 專利品
- **liquidation** 〔,lɪkwɪ'deʃən〕 *n.* 清理
- **bankrupt** 〔'bæŋkrʌpt〕 *n.* 破產
- **failure** 〔'feljɚ〕 *n.* 倒閉
- *price cutting* 削價　　*falling price* 跌價

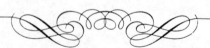

20 May I take your order? 餐飲會話

─〈會話實況〉─

餐飲部門目前已成為各大百貨公司或商店的重要附屬單位，顧客在用餐時的接待英語不同於購物時的用語，所以必須注意其中的區別，如 *order* 是**點菜**的意思，不是購物時所謂訂購的意思。

Dialogue 1

S : May I take your order? We have to let you know that *the spaghetti is sold out*.
   您要點菜了嗎？我們必須告訴您義大利麵已經賣完了。

C : Oh, I see... Then can I have sautéed pork, please?
   嗯，我看看……那麼我要一客炸豬肉。

S : Certainly. Would you like to *have a full course*?
   好的，您要全餐嗎？

C : Yes, please. 好。

Dialogue 2

S : Are you ready to order, sir? 先生，您要點菜了嗎？

C : How long will Oyster Sauce Beef take?
   蠔油牛肉要花多少時間？

S : It will be ready in, say, 10 minutes.
   差不多十分鐘就能準備好了。

C : Oh, I'll take it. 那麼，我要一客。

S : Certainly. 好的。

Dialogue 3

S : *There's a tax for bills exceeding $2,500 per person.*
超過二千五百元，每個人要加付營業稅。

C : Really? *What's the rate*? 眞的嗎？稅率是多少？

S : 10% ma'am. 百分之十，女士。

Dialogue 4

C : *Do you charge for service*? 你們收服務費嗎？

S : Yes, we do. We charge 10% of the bill for service.
是的，我們收百分之十的服務費。

Dialogue 5

C : Can I take your cakes home? 我可以把蛋糕帶走嗎？

S : Yes, certainly. 當然可以。

C : How long will they keep? 能保存多久？

S : Say, a couple of days *at the longest*, if you put them in your refrigerator, but you should eat them soon. As you know, *the sooner the better*.
如果放在冰箱裏，最多能保存幾天，不過您應該儘快把它吃掉，您也知道，愈早吃愈好。

Useful Examples

活用例句

① Would you like to *order a full-course meal* or à la carte?

① 您想叫一份全餐，還是按菜單點菜？

② Please buy *a meal ticket* first.

② 請先買餐券。

③ *May I take your order*?
Are you ready to order?

③ 您要點菜了嗎?
您準備好點菜了嗎?

④ Spaghetti *is sold out*.

④ 義大利麵已經賣完了。

⑤ The tax is 10%.

⑤ 稅率是百分之十。

⑥ *There is a tax for bills exceeding* $2,500 *per person*.

⑥ 超過兩千五百元時,每個人必須加付營業稅。

⑦ We charge 10% of the bill *for service*.

⑦ 我們收取百分之十服務費。

⑧ They (it) will only keep for a couple of days *at the longest in your refrigerator*.

⑧ 放在冰箱裏,它們(它)最多只能保存幾天。

⑨ *As you know, the sooner the better*.

⑨ 你也知道,愈早吃愈好。

⑩ Do you charge for service?

⑩ 你們收取服務費嗎?

【註】

order〔'ɔrdɚ〕*v.* 點菜   spaghetti〔spə'ɡɛtɪ〕*n.* 義大利麵條

sauté〔so'te〕*v.* 炸;煎;炒   pork〔pɔrk〕*n.* 猪肉

course〔kɔrs〕*n.* 一道菜   tax〔tæks〕*n.* 稅

bill〔bɪl〕*n.* 發票   rate〔ret〕*n.* 價格;比率

charge〔tʃɑrdʒ〕*v.*, *n.* 索價

refrigerator〔rɪ'frɪdʒə,retɚ〕*n.* 電冰箱

meal〔mil〕*n.* 一餐   á la carte〔,ɑlə'kɑrt〕*adv.* 按菜單自行點菜

餐飲專用術語

- **appetite** 〔'æpə,taɪt〕 *n.* 胃口；食慾
- *stimulate appetite* 開胃
- **nausea** 〔'nɔsɪə〕 *n.* 反胃；嘔吐
- *diet keeper* 節食　　　　　　**tip** 〔tɪp〕 *n.* 小費
- **chit** 〔tʃɪt〕 *n.* 掛帳
- *no gratuities accepted* 不收小費
- **captain** 〔'kæptɪn〕 *n.* 領班
- **chef** 〔ʃɛf〕 *n.* 主廚
- **victualler** 〔'vɪtḷə〕 *n.* 餐館老闆
- *reserved seats* 預留座位　　*one course* 一道菜
- **dessert** 〔dɪ'zɜt〕 *n.* 甜點
- **buffet** 〔'bʌfɪt〕 *n.* 自助餐
- **cafeteria** 〔,kæfə'tɪrɪə〕 *n.* 自助餐廳
- *midnight snack* 宵夜　　　*quick lunch* 快餐
- *serve up* 上菜
- **menu** 〔'menju〕 *n.* 菜單　　**bill** 〔bɪl〕 *n.* 帳單
- **hospitable** 〔'hɑspɪtəbḷ〕 *adj.* 招待週到的
- **disserve** 〔dɪs'sɜv〕 *v.* 招待不週
- *informal dinner* 便餐　　　*outside sale* 外賣

Part D

說明塲所位置
WHERE THE SITUATION IS

7 It's on the 3rd floor.
層數及建築物

<＜會話實況＞>

在百貨公司做事，身爲店員最低限度要明白每一層樓的**營業項目**，此類英語會話容易搞混，如 *It's in the first basement.* 它在地下一樓。因此必須多加練習。

Dialogue 1

C : Excuse me. 對不起，打擾一下。

S : Yes. May I help you, ma'am?
　　好的。女士，我能幫你什麼忙嗎？

C : *I'm looking for chinaware.* 我在找瓷器部門。

S : Japanese or Western? 日式還是西式的？

C : Japanese. 日式的。

S : *It's on the 5th floor.* 在五樓。

C : Thank you. 謝謝你。

S : You're welcome. 不客氣。

Dialogue 2

C : Excuse me. 對不起，打擾一下。

S : Yes. Good morning, sir. 好的。早安，先生。

C : Morning. *Where do I go for sportswear?*
　　早安。我在哪裏能買到運動裝？

S : It's in *the other* (*next*) *building.* 在隔壁那棟建築物。

C : Oh, I see. How do I get there?
　　哦，我知道了。但是我要怎麼到那裏去呢？

S : *We have a passageway on the 3rd and 5th floors.*
　　在三樓和五樓有通道。

C : Thanks. 謝謝。

S : Not at all. 不客氣。

Dialogue 3

C : *Where do you have dresses?* 你們的服裝部在哪裏？

S : We have *designer's brands* on the 4th floor, and others on the 3rd floor.
　　有設計師品牌的在四樓，其餘的在三樓。

C : Thank you. 謝謝你。

S : Not at all. 不客氣。

Dialogue 4

C : Is there a coffee shop in this store?
　　這家店裏有咖啡屋嗎？

S : Yes, there is. It's *in the 2nd basement.*
　　有，在地下室二樓。

C : Thank you. 謝謝你。

S : Not at all. 不客氣。

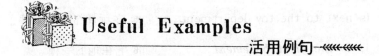

Useful Examples
活用例句

① It's on the 3rd floor.　　　　① 它在三樓。

② It's in *the annex building.*　② 那是在附屬建築裏。

③ It's in *the other building.*

③ 那是在另一棟建築物裏。

④ We have a *passageway* on the 3rd and 5th floors.

④ 在三樓和五樓有通道。

⑤ There is a passageway *upstairs* (*downstairs*).

⑤ 在樓上（樓下）有通道。

⑥ You're welcome.
Anytime.

My pleasure.
Don't mention it.

⑥ 不客氣。
不客氣。（表示隨時願意再幫助你）。
我的榮幸。
不要客氣。

⑦ It is over here.

⑦ 它在這邊。

⑧ It is over there.

⑧ 在那邊。

⑨ It is on the other side.

⑨ 在另一邊。

⑩ It is on the right side.

⑩ 在右邊。

⑪ It is on the left side.

⑪ 在左邊。

⑫ It is *in the rear.*

⑫ 在後門。

⑬ It is *in the center.*

⑬ 它在中間。

⑭ It is *in front of the* elevator.

⑭ 在電梯的前方。

⑮ It is next to the toy department.

⑮ 在玩具部門的隔壁。

⑯ It is *in the first basement.*

⑯ 它在地下一樓。

⑰ It is in the new building.

⑰ 在新大樓裏。

⑱ It is in the old building.

⑱ 在舊大樓裏。

《樓層專門術語》

- It's in the first（1st）basement.　　在地下一樓。
- It's on the first（1st）floor.　　在一樓。
- It's on the second（2nd）floor.　　在二樓。
- It's on the third（3rd）floor.　　在三樓。
- It's on the seventh（7th）floor.　　在七樓。
- It's on the rooftop.　　在屋頂。
- It's upstairs.　　在樓上。
- It's downstairs.　　在樓下。

IT'S ON THE 3ᴿᴰ FLOOR.　在三樓。

【註】

chinaware〔'tʃaɪnə,wɛr〕n. 瓷器　　sportswear〔'sports,wɛr〕n. 運動裝
passageway〔'pæsɪdʒ,we〕n. 通路；走廊　　brand〔brænd〕n. 商標；名牌
basement〔'besmənt〕n. 地下室　　annex〔'ænɛks〕n. 附屬建築
upstairs〔ʌp'stɛrz〕adv. 在樓上　　rear〔rɪr〕n. 後部；背後
rooftop〔'ruf,tɑp〕n. 屋頂

Where can I find stereos?
同樓的其他售貨處

<會話實況>

在專櫃服務時，一定要對同層樓的**其他售貨地點**及**位置圖**，有相當程度的認識，以方便指點顧客，維持營運水準。如*They're at the very end, on your left.* 在您左方的盡頭。

Dialogue 1

C : Do you have *attaché cases* on this floor?
　　在這層樓有賣公文箱的地方嗎？

S : Yes, sir. They're *at the very end*, *on your right*.
　　有的，先生。在您右手邊的盡頭。

C : Thank you. 謝謝你。

S : You're welcome. 不客氣。

Dialogue 2

C : Where is the tie department?
　　領帶部門在哪裏？

S : It's *across the floor*, *next to* the elevator.
　　穿過樓梯，電梯的隔壁。

C : Thank you. 謝謝你。

S : You're welcome. 不客氣。

Dialogue 3

C : *Where's the smoking room?*
　　吸煙室在哪裏？

S : If you *go up* the stairs, it will be *on your right.*
　　如果您走上樓，就在您的右邊。

C : Oh, don't you have one *on this floor*?
　　噢，這一層樓沒有嗎？

S : I'm sorry, but we only have a men's room on this floor.
　　很抱歉，這一層樓只有一間男士的盥洗室。

Dialogue 4

C : *Where's the elevator?* 電梯在哪裏？

S : It's *at the landing between this floor and the floor downstairs (upstairs).*
　　在這層樓和樓下（樓上）之間的階梯上。

C : *You mean* the staircase?
　　你是說樓梯間？

S : Yes, that's right. 是的。

Dialogue 5

C : *Where can I find stereos?*
　　我在哪裏能買到立體音響？

S : They're in the other corner, *on the diagonal.* (*They're across the floor, in the other corner.*)
　　在另一個角落，在斜對面。（要橫過這層樓，在另一邊。）

C : Thank you. 謝謝你。

S : Not at all. 不客氣。

Dialogue 6

C : *Where are the cameras*？照相機部門在哪裏？

S : Down this aisle, *in front of* the staircase.
　　順這條通道走下去，在樓梯間前面。

C : Thank you. 謝謝你。

S : You're welcome. 不客氣。

 Useful Examples
──────────────── 活用例句 ←←←←←←←

① It's in the center, *by the escalator.*

① 在中間，扶梯旁邊。

② We also *have a wagon sale* in the center, by the escalator.

② 我們在中間，扶梯旁拍賣嬰兒車。

③ It's *down* the hall, *on your right* (left).

③ 順著這條通道，在您的右手（左手）邊。

④ It's *down this aisle*, on your right.

④ 順著這條通道，在您的右手邊。

⑤ It's *at the very end*, on your right.

⑤ 在您右手邊的盡頭。

⑥ It's on the other side of the escalator.

⑥ 在扶梯的另一邊。

⑦ If you go straight down, you'll see a sign. At the sign turn to the left. *It's right ahead of you.*

⑦ 您直直地走，會看到一個記號，然後向左轉，它就在您正前方。

⑧ It's across the floor.

⑧ 在對面。

⑨ It's across the floor, in the other corner.

⑨ 在斜對面的角落裏。

⑩ *I'll show you there.* This way, please.

⑩ 我帶您去,請往這邊走。

⑪ It's over there.

⑪ 在那裏。

⑫ It's at the landing between this floor and the floor upstairs (downstairs).

⑫ 在這層樓和樓上(樓下)之間的階梯上。

【註】

attaché case 一種扁平的小公文箱

lavatory〔'lævə,torɪ〕*n.* 盥洗室

staircase〔'stɛr,kes〕*n.* 樓梯(間)

diagonal〔daɪ'ægən!〕*n.* 對角線

camera〔'kæmərə〕*n.* 照相機

escalator〔'ɛskə,letə〕*n.* 自動梯

ahead of 在⋯前面

elevator〔'ɛlə,vetə〕*n.* 電梯

landing〔'lændɪŋ〕*n.* 樓梯頂端的走廊

stereo〔'stɪrɪo〕*n.* 立體音響設備

aisle〔aɪl〕*n.* 通道;通路

wagon〔'wægən〕*n.* 嬰兒車

各種商店專用術語

- *large-scale department store* 巨型百貨公司
- **hypermarket** 〔'haɪpə,mɑrkɪt〕 *n.* 巨型商場
- *money-exchange* 外幣交換商店
- *famous department store* 名店百貨公司
- *maternity shop* 孕婦商店
- *ice cream parlor* 冰淇淋商店
- *carpet store* 地毯店　　　　*tailor shop* 西裝店
- *consignment store* 委託行　　*service station* 服務站
- *café* 〔kæ'fe〕 *n.* 咖啡館（= *coffee shop*）
- **nightclub** 〔'naɪt,klʌb〕 *n.* 夜總會
- **newsstand** 〔'njuz,stænd〕 *n.* 書報攤（= kiosk〔'kaɪɑsk〕）
- *record shop* 唱片行　　　　*chain store* 連鎖商店
- *copy center* 影印中心（= *xerox center*）
- **flea market**〔'fli,mɑrkɪt〕 *n.* 歐美跳蚤市場
- *lighting fixture shop* 燈飾商店
- *main store* 總店　　　　　*shopping center* 購物中心
- **bakery**〔'bekərɪ〕 *n.* 麵包店
- **contractor**〔'kɑntræktə ; kən'træktə〕 *n.* 特約商店
    （= *contractor's shop*）

3 Where's the lavatory?
洗手間方向

──<會話實況>──

　　通常被問及 *Where is the rest room*? 洗手間在哪裏？時，
通常都不說成 *Toilet* 或 *W.C.* (*water closet*)，就像中國人在客
人面前不說「廁所」一樣。一般說 *Men's room* (男)，*Ladies'
room* (女)，*Lavatory* (男女共用)；在家中則用 *bathroom*
及 *lavatory* 來表示。

Dialogue 1

C : ***Where's the ladies' room***? 女用盥洗室在哪裏？

S : If you go down the stairs, it will be ***on your left***.
　　如果您走下樓，就在您的左邊。

C : Oh. Thank you very much. 噢，眞是謝謝你。

S : You're welcome. 不客氣。

Dialogue 2

C : ***Where's the lavatory***? 洗手間怎麼走？

S : I'm sorry, we don't have any lavatory on this floor. But
　　you can find it on the first floor, ***next to*** the elevator.
　　很抱歉，我們這層樓沒有洗手間。一樓電梯旁才有。

C : You mean that is ***the only one*** in your store?
　　你是說你們公司裏面只有一間洗手間嗎？

S : I think so. 是的。

C : All right. Thanks. 好吧，謝謝。

S : *Don't mention it*. 別客氣。

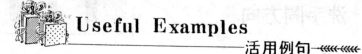

Useful Examples
活用例句 ◄◄◄◄◄◄◄

① There is one by the stairway between every floor.

每層樓之間的通道都有一處洗手間。

② This way, please. 請這邊走。

③ Would you mind stepping over here?

您介意走到這邊來嗎？

④ Please step this way.

請這邊走。

⑤ Won't you sit down? 請坐下。

⑥ Would you like to have a seat?

您不坐嗎？（請坐下。）

⑦ Please be seated over here.

請坐在那兒。

⑧ After you, ma'ma (sir).

女士（先生），您先走。

【 註 】━━━━━━━━━━━━━━━◆◆

mention 〔'mɛnʃən〕 v. 提及；注意

on one's left 在某人左方

on one's right 在某人右方

stairway 〔'stɛr,we〕 n. 樓梯

seat 〔sit〕 n. 座位；位置

房間名稱術語

- *powder*（*girl's*）*room* 女廁所（= *ladies' room*）
- kitchenet〔,kɪtʃɪn'ɛt ; -ən'ɛt〕*n.* 小厨房
- *banquet hall* 大餐廳
- *main hall* 大廳　　　　　　*dressing room* 化粧室
- nave〔nev〕*n.* 正廳　　　lounge〔laʊndʒ〕*n.* 休息室
- cloakroom〔'klok,rum〕*n.* 衣帽間
- garage〔gə'rɑdʒ〕*n.* 汽車間；車庫
- *men's room* 男廁所（= *gentlemen's room*）
- *laundry room* 洗衣室　　　*guest room* 客房

- *drawing room* 客廳　　　　*living room* 起居室
- bathroom〔'bæθ,rum ; -rʊm〕*n.* 浴室
- *reception room* 接待室　　*single room* 單人房
- storeroom〔'stor,rum〕*n.* 貯藏室（= *storage room*; *crawl space*）
- *maid's room* 傭人房（= *servants' quarters*）
- den〔dɛn〕*n.* 閱覽室（= *reading room*）
- *dining room* 餐廳
- *double room* 雙人房

What floor, sir ?
電梯內

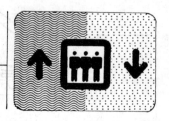

<會話實況>

在**電梯內**的服務人員，與客人接觸的時間比其他人員要短，所以在電梯內要**反應靈敏**，會話必須熟極而流，以最短的時間，達到水準以上的服務。例如：*What floor, sir* ？先生，您要到幾樓？

Dialogue 1

C : *Going up*? 上樓嗎？

S : No, down. Please *take this one over here*.
　　不，要下樓。請搭乘這邊這座電梯。

Dialogue 2

C : I want to go to the 5th floor.
　　我想到五樓。

S : We're *going straight to* the 8th floor...
　　我們直接上八樓……

C : *Non-stop*? 不停嗎？

S : Yes, that's right. So please take that one over there.
　　是的。所以請搭那邊那座電梯。

C : Thank you. 謝謝你。

S : *Not at all.* 不客氣。

Dialogue 3

C : You don't stop on the 3rd floor?

　　三樓沒有停嗎?

S : No, only on the 4th, 6th, and 8th floors, sir. ***That one will stop on your floor.*** 沒有。只有在四樓、六樓、八樓才停，先

　　生。那邊的電梯會在三樓停。

C : I see. Thank you. 我知道了。謝謝你。

S : You're welcome. 不客氣。

Dialogue 4

S : I'm sorry, ***it's full.*** Please take the next one.

　　抱歉，已經滿了，請搭下一回。

C : Oh, okay. 噢，好的。

Dialogue 5

S : We'll go back down from here.

　　我們從這裏要下降回去了。

C : Oh, then, ***how do I get to the roof*** (***rooftop***)?

　　噢，那麼，我要怎麼到頂樓呢?

S : Please take the staircase ***on your left.***

　　請走您左邊的樓梯。

C : I see. Thank you. 我知道了，謝謝。

S : You're welcome. 不客氣。

Dialogue 6

C : ***How do I get to the roof*** (***rooftop***)?

　　我要怎麼到頂樓?

S : We'll go back down from the 8th floor, so please take the staircase. It's on your left when you get out.

　　我們從八樓就要下降回去了，所以請走樓梯。走出去後就在你的左邊。

C : O.K. Thank you. 好的，謝謝。

S : Not at all. 不客氣。

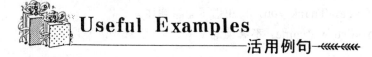

Useful Examples
活用例句→«««‹««

① *Going up* (*down*).

① 上樓（下樓）。

② We're going straight to the 8th floor.

② 我們直接上八樓。

③ We'll *stop on* the 5th, 8th, and and 9th floors.

③ 我們會在五樓、八樓和九樓停下。

④ *What floor, sir* (*ma'am*)?

④ 到幾樓，先生（女士）？

⑤ I'm sorry, (*but*) *it's full.*

⑤ 對不起，已經客滿了。

⑥ We'll go back down from here.

⑥ 我們要從這裏下降回去了。

⑦ We'll go back down from the 8th floor.

⑦ 我們要從八樓下降回去。

⑧ Please *take the staircase to* the roof (rooftop).

⑧ 請走樓梯到頂樓。

⑨ *This way* please.

⑨ 請往這兒走。

⑩ I'll *show you the way*.

⑩ 我帶路。

⑪ There's an elevator at the end of the corridor.

⑪ 走廊的盡頭有座電梯。

⑫ Walk up the stairs to the third floor.

⑫ 請走樓梯到三樓。

⑬ Please take the elevator to the fifth floor.

⑬ 請搭電梯到五樓。

⑭ *Excuse me, will it be much longer*?

⑭ 對不起,還要很久嗎?

⑮ No, just a few moments.

⑮ 不用,只要幾分鐘。

⑯ *Nothing in particular*.

⑯ 沒有特別的事。

⑰ *Let me sleep on it*.

⑰ 明天再說。

⑱ Going up, ma'ma (sir).

⑱ 女士 (先生),上樓。

⑲ Going down, ma'am (sir).

⑲ 女士 (先生),下樓。

⑳ *Please use the next elevator*.

⑳ 請搭乘下一班電梯。

㉑ This elevator will not *stop on* the fifth floor.

㉑ 電梯不會在五樓停。

【註】━━━━━━━━━◆◆

full〔fʊl〕*adj*. 裝滿的　　roof〔ruf〕*n*. 屋頂;頂樓
staircase〔'stɛr,kes〕*n*. 樓梯
elevator〔'ɛlə,vetɚ〕*n*. 電梯
escalator〔'ɛskə,letɚ〕*n*. 自動梯;電扶梯

建築物各部分名稱術語

second floor 〔美〕二樓（＝ *first floor (story)* 〔英〕）

main gate 大門   *front door* 前門

third floor 〔美〕三樓（＝ *second floor (story)* 〔英〕）

ceiling 〔'silɪŋ〕 *n.* 天花板   **door** 〔dor；dɔr〕 *n.* 門

exit 〔'ɛgzɪt；'ɛksɪt〕 *n.* 出口

basement 〔'besmənt〕 *n.* 地下室

floor 〔flor，flɔr〕 *n.* 地板   **wall** 〔wɔl〕 *n.* 牆壁

corridor 〔'kɔrədɚ；-，dɔr；'kɑr-〕 *n.* 走廊

porch 〔pɔrtʃ〕 *n.* 通道（＝〔美〕 *veranda*）

doorjamb 〔'dor,dʒæm；'dɔr-〕 *n.* 門柱

back door 後門（＝ *rear door*）

front step 前門階梯   *ridge of a roof* 屋脊

  roof 〔ruf〕 *n.* 屋頂   **eaves** 〔ivz〕 *n.* 屋簷

beam 〔bim〕 *n.* 屋樑   *spiral staircase* 廻轉梯

elevator 〔'ɛlə,vetɚ〕 *n.* 電梯（＝lift 〔lɪft〕）

escalator 〔'ɛskə,letɚ〕 *n.* 電動（轉）梯

upstairs 〔ʌp'stɛrz〕 *n.* 樓上

downstairs 〔,daʊn'stɛrz〕 *n.* 樓下；一樓（＝〔美〕*first floor*；〔英〕*ground floor*）

stairway 〔'stɛr,we〕 *n.* 樓梯

Part E

說明營業時間
BUSINESS TIME

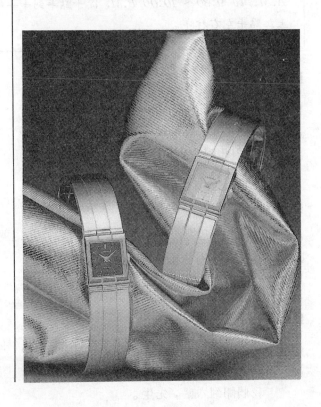

We open from 10:00 to 6:00.
平常的營業時間

＜會話實況＞

向顧客說明**營業時間**（*Business time*）的同時，最低限度也要告訴客人櫃台及厠所的方向，才能算是一項完整的服務。一般而言，台灣大部份商店及百貨公司都是 *open from 10:30 ～ 11:00 A.M. to 9:30 ～ 10:00 P.M.* 從十點半到十一點開始營業，至晚上九點半左右打烊。

Dialogue 1

C : What time does your store *open*?
　　你們店幾點開始營業？

S : *We open at 10:00*, sir.
　　我們十點鐘開始營業，先生。

Dialogue 2

C : What's *your closing time*? 你們幾點打烊？

S : That's (It's) 6:00, ma'am.
　　六點，女士。

Dialogue 3

C : How late are you open？ 你們開到多晚？

S : We're open till 6:00, sir.
　　我們開到六點，先生。

Dialogue 4

C : You're open *from what time to what time*?
　　你們幾點到幾點營業？

S : We're open from 10:00 to 6:00, sir.
　　我們從十點營業到六點，先生。

Dialogue 5

C : *What're your business hours*? 你們營業時間是什麼時候？

S : From 10:00 to 6:00, ma'am. 從十點到六點，女士。

Dialogue 6

C : Are you open at 9:30 a.m. (*8:00 p.m.*)?
　　你們上午九點半（下午8點）開始營業嗎？

S : No, I'm sorry. We're not open *that early* (*late*).
　　抱歉，不是的。我們沒有那麼早（晚）開始。

 **Useful Examples**
―――活用例句→«««‹«««

① *We are open from* 10:00 *to* 6:00. 我們從十點營業到六點。
　(= *Our store is open from* 10:00 *to* 6:00.
　= *Our business hours are from* 10:00 *to* 6:00.

② We open (*close*) at 9:00. 我們九點開始營業（打烊）。

③ *How late* are you open? 你們營業到幾點？

④ What're your business hours? 你們的營業時間從幾點到幾點?

⑤ You're open *from what time to what time*?
　　你們從幾點到幾點營業？

地　名	公務機關 周一~五	公務機關 周六	私人企業 周一~五	私人企業 周六	銀行 周一~五	銀行 周六
大韓民國 Korea	9:00-18:00	9:00-13:00	10:00-17:00	10:00-14:00	10:00-17:00	9:30-13:30
日本 Japan	9:00-17:30	9:00-12:00	9:00-17:30	9:00-12:00	9:00-15:30	9:00-12:00
比利時 Belgium	9:00-13:00 14:30 15:30	OFF	8:30-12:00 14:00-17:30	OFF	9:00-13:00 14:30-16:30	OFF
丹麥 Denmark	mon-fri 10:00-15:00 9:30-18:00	OFF	8:30-12:00 13:00-16:30	OFF	9:30-18:00	OFF
中華民國 The Republic of China	9:00-17:30	9:00-12:00	9:00-17:30	9:00-12:00	9:00-15:30	9:00-12:00
印尼 Indonesia	mon-fri 8:00-15:00 thu 8:00-11:30	8:00-14:00	mon-thu 8:00-16:00 fri 9:00-11:00	8:00-12:00	8:00-12:00 8:30-13:00	8:00-11:30
印度 India	10:00-17:30	10:00-17:00	10:00-17:30	10:00-17:30	10:00-15:00	OFF
加拿大 Canada	8:30-16:30	OFF	9:00-17:00	OFF	9:00-15:00	OFF
西班牙 Spain	9:00-17:00	OFF	9:00-13:00 16:00-19:00	OFF	9:00-14:00	9:00-14:00
西德 West Germany	8:30-13:00	OFF	8:30-16:00 8:30-17:30	OFF	8:30-13:00 14:30-16:00	OFF
沙烏地阿拉伯 Saudi Arabia	8:30-13:00 17:00-20:00	fri OFF	8:30-12:30 16:30-20:00	OFF	sat-thu 8:00-13:00	fri OFF
希臘 Greece	7:30-13:30	OFF	8:00-16:00	OFF	8:00-14:00	9:00-13:00
阿拉伯聯合大公國 United Arab Emirates	sat-wed 8:00-14:00 thu 8:00-12:00	fri OFF sun 8:00-13:00	8:30-13:00 16:00-18:00	fri OFF sun 8:30-18:00	8:00-12:00 8:00-11:00	10:00-12:00
法國 France	9:00-12:00 16:00-18:00	OFF	9:00-12:00 14:00-18:00	OFF	9:00-16:00	OFF
洛杉磯 Los Angeles	8:30-17:30	OFF	9:00-17:00	OFF	10:00-15:00	OFF
科威特 Kuwait	sat-wed 7:30-13:00 thu 7:30-11:30	fri OFF	7:30-13:30	fri OFF	sat-thu 8:00-12:00	fri OFF

英國 England	9:00-17:30	OFF	9:30-17:30	OFF	9:30-15:30	OFF
香港 Hong Kong	9:00-13:00 14:00-17:00	9:00-12:00	9:00-13:00 14:00-17:00	9:00-13:00	9:00-15:00	9:39-12:00
南斯拉夫 Yugoslavia	8:00-15:00	OFF	7:00-15:00	OFF	7:00-15:00	OFF
紐西蘭 New Zealand	9:00-17:00	OFF	9:00-17:00	OFF	10:00-16:00	OFF
馬來西亞 Malaysia	8:00-16:15	8:00-12:45	8:00-16:15	8:00-12:45	10:00-15:00	9:00-11:00
紐約 New York	8:30-17:30	OFF	8:30-17:30	OFF	9:00-15:00	OFF
夏威夷 Hawaii	8:00-16:00 8:30-16:30	OFF	8:00-16:00 8:30-16:30	OFF	9:00-15:00 10:00-16:00	OFF
挪威 Norway	8:00-15:45	OFF	8:00-15:00	OFF	9:00-15:30	OFF
泰國 Thailand	8:30-16:30	OFF	8:00-17:00	OFF	9:00-15:30	OFF
華盛頓 Washington D.C.	8:30-17:30	OFF	9:00-17:00	OFF	9:00-15:00	OFF
荷蘭 Holland	9:00-17:00	OFF	※	※	9:00-16:00	OFF
菲律賓 The Philippines	9:00-12:00 13:00-17:00	OFF	9:00-13:00 13:00-17:00	OFF	9:00-15:00	9:00-12:00
瑞士 Switzerland	8:30-16:30 fri(18:00)	8:00-12:00	9:00-12:00 14:00-18:30	8:00-12:00	8:15-18:00 8:15-16:30	OFF
義大利 Italy	8:00-14:00	OFF	9:00-13:00 15:00-19:30	OFF	8:30-13:30	OFF
新加坡 Singapore	8:30-17:00	8:30-13:00	9:00-17:00	9:00-13:00	10:00-15:00	9:30-11:30
瑞典 Sweden	9:00-17:00	OFF	8:30-13:30 16:00-19:00	OFF	8:00 9:00-15:00	OFF
澳洲 Australia	9:00-17:00	OFF	9:00-17:00	OFF	9:30-16:00 10:00-17:00	OFF
蘇聯 USSR	9:00-12:00 13:00-18:00	OFF	9:00-12:00 13:00-18:00	OFF	9:00-13:00 14:00-20:00	OFF

Our restaurants are open till 8:00.
不同的營業時間

─────<會話實況>─────

近來百貨公司十分流行在地下樓設置**食品街**，或**超級市場**，由於產品性質不同，所以營業時間並**不同於**其他部門，店員在向顧客解說營業時間時須注意此點，以免顧客徒勞往返。如：*Those on the 7th floor are open till 8:00.* 七樓的部門營業到八點。

Dialogue 1

C : What time do your restaurants close?

你們餐廳何時打烊？

S : ***Those on the 7th floor*** are open till 8:00, but ***others*** close at 6:00.

七樓的餐廳開到八點，但是其他的六點打烊。

Dialogue 2

C : ***The whole store*** will close at 6:00?

整個店六點就要打烊了嗎？

S : No, ma'am. Our basement is open till 7:00 because we have food departments, and the eighth floor is open till 8:00 because we have restaurants there.

不是，女士。我們地下樓因為有食品部門所以開到七點，八樓有餐廳所以開到八點。

Dialogue 3

C : *How late is your basement open*? 你們地下樓開到什麼時候？

S : It's open till 7:00, sir. 開到七點，先生。

Dialogue 4

C : *How late can I eat*? 我可以吃到什麼時候？

S : Our restaurants on the seventh floor are open till 8:00, ma'am. 我們七樓的餐廳開到八點，女士。

C : All of them? 全部嗎？

S : Yes, all of them. 是的，全部。

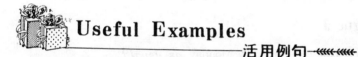 **Useful Examples**
──────────── 活用例句 ◄◄◄◄◄◄◄◄

① Our basement is open till 12:00 because we have *food departments* there.

我們地下樓營業到十二點，因為那裏有食品部門。

② Our food departments *in the basement* are open till 1:00.

我們地下樓食品街營業到一點。

③ Our 9th floor is open till 10:00 because we have restaurants there. 我們九樓營業到十點，因為那裏有餐廳。

④ Our restaurants on the 9th floor are open till 12:00.

我們九樓的餐廳營業到十二點。

⑤ *The whole store will close at 6:00*?

整個店六點鐘就要打烊嗎？

【註】━━━━━━━━━━━━━━◆◆

restaurant〔'rɛstərənt〕*n*. 飯店；餐館　　department〔dɪ'pɑrtmənt〕*n*. 部門

3

We're open everyday during the year-end gift season.
旺季的營業日

> ＜會話實況＞
>
> 　　在一年的**歲末**及**中元**時節是百貨公司的兩大**旺季**，每家商店必然照常營業以服務顧客，締造業績。在此階段店員要懂得如何向客人解說：*We're open everyday during the year-end gift season.* 我們在歲末送禮期間天天營業。

Dialogue 1

C : Are you closed next Monday *as usual*?

　　下星期一你們照常休假嗎？

S : No, ma'am. We're open 7 days a week *during the summer gift season* till *the middle of this month*.

　　不，女士。夏天送禮季節，我們每週營業七天，直到這個月中旬。

Dialogue 2

C : *When's your regular holiday*?

　　你們例假日是那一天？

S : Thursday, sir. But *the exceptions* are the summer gift season and year-end (=*Christmas*) gift season. Our store is open everyday *during those periods*.

　　星期四，先生。但是在夏季及歲末送禮季節例外。在這些期間，我們的店每天都營業。

Useful Examples
─────活用例句─

① We're open everyday during the year-end.

① 在歲末期間我們每天營業。

② Our store's open *7 days a week during the* summer gift season.

② 在夏季送禮期間，我們的店每天營業。

③ *The exceptions* are the summer-gift season and year-end gift season.

③ 夏季和歲末送禮季節時例外。

④ Are you closed on Tuesdays *as usual*?

④ 你們照例在星期二休業嗎？

⑤ This warm weather is *exceptional* for January.

⑤ 這樣熱的天氣在正月是很異常的。

⑥ I *take exception to* your statement that I am bad-tempered.

⑥ 我反對你說我脾氣不好。

⑦ Would you care to custom-make a pair of evening shoes?
（*to custom-make* 是不定詞）

⑦ 您要不要定做一雙晚宴穿的鞋子呢？

⑧ The cashier will give you *a sales slip*.

⑧ 出納員會給你一張購物清單。

⑨ Thank you for *shopping in our store*.

⑨ 謝謝光臨。

⑩ Yes, goods purchased in this store are refundable within seven days.

⑩ 是的，在本店購物，可在七天內退回。

⑪ These wool and cashmere sweaters *are from* England.

⑪ 這些羊毛及開斯米爾毛衣是英國貨。

⑫ Would you like to see our *ready-mades*?

⑫ 要不要看看成衣？

⑬ Our firm has very *favourable purchase terms.*

⑬ 我們公司有很優惠的購買辦法。

⑭ We also have cheaper ones, but they're not as good. *They are imitations.*

⑭ 便宜的我們也有，但那是仿製品，品質較差。

gift〔gɪft〕*n.* 禮物　　middle〔'mɪdl̩〕*n.* 中間
exception〔ɪk'sɛpʃən〕*n.* 例外
summer gift time 中元時節
year-end〔'jɪr, ɛnd〕*n.* 年終；年底
period〔'pɪrɪəd〕*n.* 一段時間
exceptional〔ɪk'sɛpʃənl̩〕*adj.* 特別的；異常的
statement〔'stetmənt〕*n.* 陳述；聲明
bad-tempered〔'bæd'tɛmpəd〕*adj.* 脾氣壞的；易發脾氣的

4 Our regular holiday is Thursday.
公休

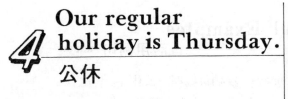

<會話實況>

　　當顧客問：你們明天公休嗎？不可以只回答：*No.* 不。必須向顧客詳細解釋商店或公司何時**例假**，何時正常營業，以給顧客便利為尚。如：*Our regular holiday is Monday.* 我們通常星期一公休。

Dialogue 1

C : Are you open tomorrow? 你們明天有沒有營業？

S : No, ma'am. I'm sorry. We're closed **on Wednesdays**.
　　沒有，夫人。很抱歉。我們每星期三休假。

Dialogue 2

C : When's your **business holiday**?
　　你們定期公休是那一天？

S : Our **regular holiday** is Thursday.
　　我們星期四定期公休。

Dialogue 3

C : When's your regular holiday? 你們公休是那一天？

S : Wednesday, ma'am. But we're open this week because it's **a national holiday**.
　　星期三，女士。但是這個星期我們有營業，因為那天是國定假日。

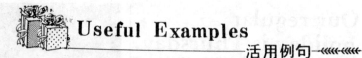

Useful Examples

活用例句→≪≪≪‧≪≪

① We're closed on Mondays. 我們每星期一公休。

　Our regular holiday is Monday. 我們每星期一公休。

② Monday is our regular holiday. 星期一是我們的例假日。

③ It is from ten, sir（ma'am）.

　先生（女士），從十點開始。

④ We're open until six, ma'am（sir）.

　女士（先生），我們營業到六點。

⑤ *Our business hours* are from ten to six.

　我們的營業時間是從十點到六點。

⑥ *We are not open for business on Fridays.*

　每週五我們休業。

【註】─────────◆

　regular holiday 例假

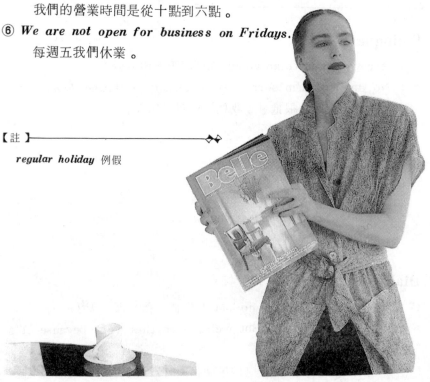

中國節日術語

中元節〔陰曆7月15日〕　*Ghost Festival*

中秋節〔陰曆8月15日〕　*Mid-Autumn（moon）Festival*

中華民國開國紀念日〔1月1日〕　*Founding Anniversary of the Republic of China*

元宵節〔陰曆1月15日〕　*Lantern Festival*

父親節〔8月8日〕　*Father's Day*

光復節〔10月25日〕　*Taiwan Restoration Day*

行憲紀念日〔12月25日〕　*Constitution Day*

青年節〔3月29日〕　*Youth Day*

兒童節〔4月4日〕　*Children's Day*

重陽節〔陰曆9月9日〕　*Double Ninth Festival*

春節〔陰曆正月初一〕　*Spring Festival*

清明節〔4月5日〕　*Tomb Sweeping Day*

教師節〔9月28日〕　*Teacher's Day（= Confucius' Birthday）*

陰曆年〔農曆1月1日〕　*Lunar New Year*

陽曆年〔1月1日〕　*Solar（western）New Year*

端午節〔陰曆5月5日〕　*Dragon Boat Festival*

雙十節〔10月10日〕　*Double-Tenth Day*

西洋節日術語

- 一百年紀念　**centennial** 〔sɛnˈtɛnɪəl〕
- 二百年紀念　**bicentennial** 〔ˌbaɪsɛnˈtɛnɪəl〕
- 三百年紀念　**tercentennial** 〔ˌtɝsɛnˈtɛnɪəl〕
- 五十週年紀念　**jubilee** 〔ˈdʒublɪˌi〕
- 公衆假日　*public holiday*　　花季　*flower season*
- 年節　**festival** 〔ˈfɛstəvḷ〕　紀念日　*memorial day*
- 除夕　*New Year's Eve*
- 假日　**holiday** 〔ˈhɑləˌde〕; *day off*
- 國定假日　*statutory holiday* (= *legal holiday*)
- 勝利紀念日　*Victory Day*　節日　*feast day* (= *holiday*)
- 節慶　*a festival*　　新年　*the New Year*
- 母親節〔5月第2個禮拜天〕*Mother's Day*
- 美獨立紀念日〔7月4日〕*Independence Day*
- 婦女節〔3月8日〕*Women's Day*
- 復活節〔3月21日，按卽春分〕*Easter Sunday*
- 感恩節〔11月第4個星期四〕*Thanksgiving Day*
- 萬聖節〔11月1日〕*All Saints' Day*; *Halloween Day*
- 聖誕節〔12月25日〕*Christmas Day*
- 情人(范倫泰)節〔2月14日〕(*St.*) *Valentine's Day*
- 愚人節〔4月1日〕*April Fool's Day*

Part F

更進一步的溝通
FURTHER COMMUNICATION

7 Hold the line, please.
總機之電話應對

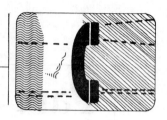

<> ＜會話實況＞

　　顧客和百貨部門常常需要藉著電話中的應對來解決問題，**總機**是其中最重要的一環，它是迅速**處理各種抱怨、詢問**以及**誤解**的中間站，因此，總機必須具備良好的服務態度及流利有禮的談吐。幫客人**轉**電話前要說：*Hold the line, please.* 請稍等。

Dialogue 1

C : I'd like to speak to Mr. Chen of your Toy Department.
　　我想和你們玩具部的陳先生說話。

O : *Hold the line, please...* I'm sorry but *the line is busy at the moment.* Would you like to wait or *call back later*?
　　請稍候……，抱歉，現在正通話中。你要不要等一下或者稍候再撥？

C : I'll hold, then. 我等一下。

O : Thank you... The line is open now, so *we'll put you through... Go ahead, please.*
　　謝謝你……，現在線路通了，我們會幫你接通……。請開始。

Dialogue 2

C : *Who should I talk to if I have complaints*?
　　我應找誰抱怨呢？

O : We'll *put* you *through to* our Complaint Department.
　　我們會幫你接到控訴部門。

Dialogue 3

C : Last week I bought a sweater from your store, but *it's already coming loose.*

　　上週我在你們店裏買了一件毛衣，但是它已經變鬆了。

O : I see, hold the line, please. We'll put you through to our department *in charge.*

　　我知道了，請稍候。我們會幫你接到負責的部門。

Dialogue 4

C : Is this the President Department?

　　是大統百貨公司嗎？

O : *Speaking.* (*Yes, it is.*) May I help you?

　　是的。能爲您效勞嗎？

C : Yes. Could you put me through to the Toy Department?

　　請幫我轉玩具部好嗎？

O : Certainly, sir. Just a moment, please.

　　好的，先生。請稍候。

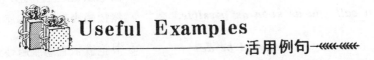

Useful Examples

━━━━━━━━━━━━━━━━━━━活用例句→≪≪≪≪≪

① *Hold the line, please.*

② *Go ahead, please.*

③ We are sorry, but *the line is busy at the moment.*

④ Who would you like to speak to?

① 請稍等（別掛斷）。

② 請開始通話。

③ 很抱歉，現在正通話中。

④ 請問你要找那一位？

⑤ Would you like to *wait or call back later*?

⑤ 你要等一下或者待會再打過來？

⑥ We're now calling the Men's Formal Department on the fourth floor.

⑥ 我們正打電話到四樓的紳士部門。

⑦ We're sorry. It was our mistake.

⑦ 抱歉。這是我們的錯。

⑧ We're sorry. *It was our fault.*

⑧ 抱歉。這是我們的過失。

⑨ We're sorry. *We will exchange* it.

⑨ 很抱歉。我們會幫您換。

⑩ We're sorry. *We will refund you.*

⑩ 抱歉。我們會把錢退還給您。

⑪ We're sorry. Shall we exchange it?

⑪ 抱歉。我們可以退換嗎？

⑫ We're sorry. We will check it, and *call you as soon as possible.*

⑫ 很抱歉。我們會查查看，然後儘快打電話給您。

⑬ We're sorry. *It should be delivered* in a few days.

⑬ 很抱歉。它應該過幾天就會送到。

⑭ *We regret the inconvenience*, but it was unintentional *on our part.*

⑭ 很遺憾有此不便，但我們是無心的。

⑮ I'm sure he (she) *made an unintentional error.*

⑮ 我確定他（她）是犯了無心之過。

⑯ We're sorry, but we can't help it.

⑯ 很抱歉，但我們實在沒辦法。

⑰ We're sorry. It was *because of our poor communication.*

⑰ 很抱歉。這是由於我們缺乏溝通所致。

⑱ We're sorry, *we couldn't explain it satisfactorily.*

⑱ 抱歉不能給您滿意的答覆。

⑲ It's unbelievable.

⑲ 眞不敢相信。

⑳ We're sorry, but that is about all we can do.

⑳ 很抱歉，我們所能做的大概就是這些了。

㉑ We're sorry, we didn't know *such a thing would happen.*

㉑ 很抱歉，我們不知道會發生這種事。

㉒ We're sorry, but *we can't guarantee it in such a case.*

㉒ 很抱歉，在這種情形下，我們不能保證。

㉓ It couldn't possibly be.

㉓ 這是不可能的。

㉔ We're sorry we can't because *it is against our regulation.*

㉔ 很抱歉我們不能這樣做，因爲這樣做是違反規定的。

㉕ We'll put you through to our department in charge.

㉕ 我們會替您接通負責的部門。

㉖ We're sorry to *have kept you waiting.*
Thank you for waiting.

㉖ 抱歉讓您久等。

【註】━━━━━━━━━━━━━━◆◆

hold the line 請勿掛斷　　　***go ahead*** 繼續；去做

complaint〔kəm'plent〕*n.* 訴苦；控訴

loose〔lus〕*adj.* 寬鬆的　　line〔laın〕*n.* 線路

mistake〔mə'stek〕*n.* 錯誤；誤解　　fault〔fɔlt〕*n.* 過失；錯誤

exchange〔ıks'tʃendʒ〕*v.,n.* 交換；調換

refund〔'ri,fʌnd〕*n.* 退款

inconvenience〔,ınkən'vinjəns〕*n.* 不便；困難

unintentional〔,ʌnın'tɛnʃənḷ〕*adj.* 無心的；非故意的

error〔'ɛrɚ〕*n.* 錯誤

communication〔kə,mjunə'keʃən〕*n.* 傳達消息、思想、意見等

explain〔ık'splen〕*v.* 解釋；辯解

satisfactorily〔,sætıs'fæktərılı〕*adv.* 滿意地；圓滿地

unbelievable〔,ʌnbı'livəbḷ〕*adj.* 不可信的；不能令人相信的

guarantee〔,gærən'ti〕*v.* 保證；擔保

against〔ə'gɛnst〕*prep.* 反對；逆

regulation〔,rɛgjə'leʃən〕*n.* 規定；條例

He is out at the moment.
櫃枱之電話應對

─<會話實況>─

　　各**專櫃**人員如果不懂英文，一旦接到外國人打來的電話，務必鎮定，隨時準備說 *Excuse me*？對不起。讓眞正懂英文的人來接聽。

Dialogue 1

C : Could I speak to a Mr. Suzuki, please?
　　請找鈴木先生聽電話好嗎？

S : I'm sorry, but he's *out for lunch* right now.
　　抱歉，他正好出去吃中飯了。

C : Oh, really? What time will he be back?
　　噢，眞的嗎？他什麼時候會回來？

S : He'll be back by 1:30. *Is there anything I can do for you*?
　　他一點半會回來。還要我幫什麼忙嗎？

C : Um, I just want to *know if my pants are ready*.
　　嗯，我只是想知道我的褲子好了沒有。

S : May I have your name, please?
　　請問貴姓大名？

C : Jones. Mr. Richard Jones.
　　瓊斯。理查‧瓊斯先生。

S : ***Hold the line, please...*** I'm sorry to have kept you waiting. Yes, they're ready. Tomorrow is our ***regular holiday***,
   so we'll be waiting for you anytime today or ***from*** Friday
   on.

   請稍候。……抱歉讓您久等。您的褲子好了。但明天我們公休，
   所以請您今天或者星期五以後隨時來拿。

C : I see. Thank you very much.

   我知道了。非常謝謝你。

S : Not at all. Thank you. ***Have a nice day.***

   不客氣。謝謝。祝你有愉快的一天。

Dialogue 2

S : Hello. This is F.M. Station Department in Taipei. May I
   speak to Mrs. Thompson, please?

   喂。這裏是台北的流行頻道百貨公司。請找湯普森太太聽電話。

C : Oh, she's not home now.

   噢，她現在不在家。

S : What time will she be back?

   她什麼時候回來？

C : I don't know, but she said she was coming home late.
   Shall I take your message?

   我不知道，但是她說過會晚一點回家。你要留話嗎？

S : Yes, please. We'd like to let her know that ***her purchase
   on order*** has arrived, so we'll be waiting for her anytime
   after tomorrow. Tomorrow is our business holiday.

   好的。請轉告她，她訂購的東西已經送來了，後天我們隨時等她
   來。因明天是我們的休業日。

C : I see. That's all? 我知道了。就這樣嗎？

S : Yes, that's all. 是的，就這樣。

C : O.K. I'll tell her that. ***Thank you for calling.***

　　好的。我會告訴她。謝謝你打電話來。

S : Thank you. Good-bye.

　　謝謝。再見。

 # Useful Examples
───────────────────── 活用例句 ◄◄◄◄ ◄◄◄

① *He* (*she*) ***is off today.*** 他（她）今天休假。

② He (she) is ***out for lunch*** right now.

　　他（她）現在正好出去吃中飯。

③ He (she) is out ***at the moment.***

　　他（她）現在不在。

④ He (she) is ***on another line*** right now.

　　他（她）現在正在電話中。

⑤ He (she) will be back ***in five minutes.***

　　他（她）五分鐘後會回來。

⑥ ***Is there anything I can do for you?***

　　有沒有需要我為您效勞的地方？

⑦ Speaking. 我就是。

【註】━━━━━━━━━━━━━━ ◆◆

for lunch 吃中飯　　pants〔pænts〕*n. pl.* 褲子

message〔'mɛsɪdʒ〕*n.* 消息；傳言；口信

purchase〔'pɝtʃəs〕*n.* 購買（之物）

purchase on order 訂購之物　　arrive〔ə'raɪv〕*v.* 抵達；來臨

off〔ɔf; ɑf〕*adj.* 休閒的；不工作的

Hello. Would you mind speaking more slowly ? 其他之電話應對

─<會話實況>─

　　電話中的英文因爲看不到對方的表情等，所以聽起來特別難懂。而且在毫無心理準備的情況下忽然聽見 *Hello*（喂），則也有慌張地連一句話也不會說的情形出現。這樣一來對方會以爲電話沒打通，而一直說 *Hello, Hello*（喂，喂……）。像這種情況務必要沈著下來，妥爲應對，以免大損公司形象。

Dialogue 1

C : Hello. Is this TATUNG Corporation?

　　喂，這裏是大同公司嗎？

O : Speaking. May I help you?

　　是的。能爲您效勞嗎？

C : Yes. Could you *page* Mr. Je Huang *for* me?

　　請幫我廣播黃傑先生來接電話好嗎？

O : Certainly, sir. Where do you think he will be?

　　好的，先生。您認爲他會在哪裏呢？

C : He's probably having lunch. Could you page the restaurants, please?

　　他可能在吃中飯。請向餐廳呼叫好嗎？

O : O.K. *I'll do that.*

　　好的。我會照辦。

Dialogue 2

C : Can you please *connect me with the export department*?

　　請幫我接出口部好嗎？

O : Hold the line a moment, I'll connect you.

　　別掛斷，我幫您接。

Dialogue 3

C : Would you please *transfer* me *to* the production department?

　　請幫我轉到產品部好嗎？

O : *I'll put you through.* 好的。

C : Thanks. 謝謝。

Dialogue 4

C : This is Mr. Agnelli. Would you please *put me through to* Mr. Yeh, please?

　　我是艾格納理。請幫我接葉先生好嗎？

O : I'm sorry, he's out at the moment. Would you like to talk to someone else in the same section?

　　抱歉，他現在出去了。要不要和同部門的其他職員通話？

Dialogue 5

C : Hello. I want to know *the price of* the large Webster's Dictionary.

　　喂。我想知道大本韋氏辭典一本多少錢。

O : Hold the line, please. I'll *connect you with the Foreign Book Department.*

　　請稍候別掛。我替你接外國圖書部門。

C : All right. 好的。

O : Foreign Book Department. 外國圖書部。

C : What is the price of the large Webster's Dictionary？
大本韋氏辭典一本多少錢？

O : It's $800, sir. 八百元，先生。

C : Do you give a discount if we buy it *in large quantities*？
如果我們大量訂購，有沒有打折？

O : *How many copies, sir*? 要幾本，先生？

C : Oh, a dozen or two. 哦，一打或兩打。

O : *In that case*, we can't give a discount, I'm sorry to say.
Our rule is to *give no rebate* for the purchase of less
than 50 copies *at one time*, sir.

對不起，那樣的話我們不能打折。我們規定一次買少於 50 本時
不打折扣。

C : Well, we don't need that many now. *Thank you just the
same.*

嗯，我們現在不需要那麼多。還是要謝謝您。

O : Thank you very much. 非常謝謝。

Useful Examples

活用例句 ◂◂◂◂◂◂

① Just a moment, please.

① 請稍候。

② *Hang on*, please.

② 請稍等。

③ Would you mind speaking more slowly?

③ 您可不可以講慢一點？

④ May I ask *who is this*, please?

④ 請問哪裏找？

⑤ May I know who is calling?

⑤ 請問哪裏找？

⑥ May I have your *first name*?

⑥ 請問您的大名？

⑦ Is this your *last* (*family*) *name*?

⑦ 請問您貴姓？

⑧ May I have your *full name*?

⑧ 請問您貴姓大名？

⑨ *Would you mind spelling your name*?

⑨ 請您拼出您的名字好嗎？

⑩ *He* (*She*) *is not in now.*

⑩ 他（她）現在不在。

⑪ He (She) is *off* today.

⑪ 他（她）今天休息。

⑫ He (She) is busy right now.

⑫ 他（她）現在正在忙。

⑬ He (She) is *on a business trip* now.

⑬ 他（她）目前正在出差。

⑭ I will have him (her) *call you soon*.

⑭ 我會讓他（她）儘快打電話給您。

⑮ I will have him (her) *get in touch with* you.

⑮ 我會讓他（她）跟您聯絡。

⑯ Do you mean you want to *cancel your order*?

⑯ 您是說您想要取消您的訂購？

⑰ Do you mean it isn't delivered yet?

⑰ 您的意思是它還沒有送去嗎？

⑱ Do you mean *it was mistaken*?

⑱ 您的意思是它搞錯了？

⑲ Do you mean you want him to call you back?

⑲ 您是說要他給您回電嗎？

⑳ *Please dial zero first.*

⑳ 請先撥 0 。

㉑ We're sorry, this is an *internal* phone. Please use the telephone over there.

㉑ 很抱歉，這是內線電話。請用那邊那支電話。

㉒ Please use *the public telephone* near the elevator (stairway).

㉒ 請使用電梯(樓梯)附近的公共電話。

㉓ Please use this telephone.

㉓ 請用這支電話。

㉔ *May I have* your phone number?

㉔ 請您留下您的電話號碼好嗎？

㉕ I will *call* you *back* later.

㉕ 待會我會回電給您。

㉖ What time do you expect him (her) back?

㉖ 您希望他（她）幾點回來？

㉗ May I *have a message*?

㉗ 我能留話嗎？

㉘ I will check it, and call you *as soon as possible*.

㉘ 我會查查看，再儘快給您電話。

㉙ He is *on another line* now.

㉙ 他現在正在電話中。

㉚ Will you *give* us *a call*, please?

㉚ 您可以給我們電話嗎？

㉛ There is no one *by the name of* Conrad here.

㉛ 這裏沒有這個名叫康拉德的人。

㉜ Shall I (we) tell him to call you back?

㉜ 要不要我告訴他回您電話？

㉝ Would you like to *leave a message*?

㉝ 您要不要留話？

㉞ *Would you mind calling again*?

㉞ 請您再打一次好嗎？

㉟ May I ask *who's calling*?

㉟ 請問您是那一位？

㊱ *How do you spell your name, please*?

㊱ 請問您的名字怎麼寫？

㊲ May I speak to Mr./ Mrs./ Miss/ Ms. Hsieh, please?

㊲ 請找謝先生（女士，小姐）。

㊳ What time will he (she) be back?

㊳ 他（她）什麼時候會回來？

㊴ We'd like to let you know that your *purchase on order* has arrived (come).

㊴ 我們是想要通知您，您訂購的東西已經來了。

⑩ We'd like to *inform* you that your sweater is ready.

We'd like to *inform* you that your belt has come back.

⑩ 我是要通知您，您的毛衣已經好了。

我是要通知您，您的皮帶已經回來了。

㊶ We'll be waiting for you *anytime*.

㊶ 我們隨時等候您。

㊷ *Thank you for calling.*

㊷ 謝謝你打電話來。

㊸ Could I speak to a Mr. Suzuki, please?

㊸ 請您找一位鈴木先生好嗎？

Webster〔'wɛbstɚ〕*n.* 韋伯斯特（Noah Webster 美國辭典編輯家）

connect one with~（把電話）接到

give a discount 打折　　quantity〔'kwɑntətɪ〕*n.* 數量

copy〔'kɑpɪ〕*n.*（書籍等）一本

dozen〔'dʌzn̩〕*n.* 一打　　*in that case* 那樣的話

rebate〔rɪ'bet〕*n.* 折扣

purchase〔'pɚtʃəs〕*n.* 購買

cancel〔'kænsl̩〕*v.* 取消；作廢

dial〔'daɪəl〕*v.* 撥電話號碼　　zero〔'zɪro〕*n.* 零；0

internal〔ɪn'tɚnl̩〕*adj.* 內在的；內部的

public〔'pʌblɪk〕*adj.* 公共的；公用的

inform〔ɪn'fɔrm〕*v.* 通知；報告

4 Do you have the receipt?

退貨、退錢、換貨的詢問

> **＜會話實況＞**
>
> 　　商品一旦賣出，必然要有良好的**售後服務**來應付客人有關**退錢**、
> **換貨**、**退貨**等的詢問，此時，要注意的是顧客手上是否持有**收據**或
> **發票**，並且要確認商品的原售價及標籤。委婉地說：*I'm sorry I*
> *cannot refund you because of our store rule.* 很抱歉我不能
> 退給您錢，因為這是我們公司的規定。

Dialogue 1

C : I bought this here yesterday, but it was too small for me,
　　 so I want *a size bigger*.

　　 昨天我在這裏買了這個，但是，我穿起來太小了，所以我想要尺
　　 寸大一點的。

S : Oh, I see. *But we can't exchange it.*

　　 噢，我知道了。可是我們不能換給您。

C : Why not?

　　 為什麼不行？

S : Because *we treat it the same as* lingerie *once* you have
　　 opened it.

　　 因為一旦您打開它，我們就視同女用內衣一般，概不退換。

C : O.K. I'll pay for a new one.

　　 好吧。我再買新的。

Dialogue 2

C : I bought it here yesterday, but it broke already.

我昨天在這裏買了這個，但是已經壞了。

S : *What happened*?

怎麼回事？

C : I don't know. But it stopped *all of a sudden*.

我不知道。但是它突然不動了。

S : May I see it, please?... Did you drop this or something?
Because there's a crack here, you see.

請讓我看看……你是不是弄掉了什麼東西？因爲這裏有道裂縫，
您看。

C : No, I didn't. Anyway, can you exchange this for a new
one?

沒有，我沒弄掉。無論如何，可不可以換個新的？

S : Do you have *proof* that you bought it here?

您能證明您是在這裏買的嗎？

C : Sure. I have *the receipt. Will that do*?

當然。我有收據。這可以嗎？

S : Certainly. Just a moment, please. *We're very sorry for
the trouble* (*inconvenience*).

當然，請稍等。很抱歉讓您這麼麻煩（造成您的不便）。

Dialogue 3

C : I bought this here some minutes ago, but *I've changed my
mind*. I want that one instead.

幾分鐘以前我買了這個，但是我改變主意了。我想要那一個。

S : Certainly, ma'am. Just a moment, please... I'm sorry to have kept you waiting. *I'm afraid they're not the same price* so *the balance* is NT$ 300.

好的，女士。請稍等……很抱歉讓您久等了。恐怕它們的價錢不同，所以您還得再付台幣三百元。

C : All right, here you are.

沒關係，拿去。

S : Thank you very much. Please come again.

非常謝謝您。請再度光臨。

Dialogue 4

C : I bought this yesterday, but it's too small for me. *I can't fit into it.*

我昨天買了這個，但是太小了。我穿不下。

S : I see. Would you like a size bigger?

我明白了。您要尺寸大一點的嗎？

C : I guess so. Yeah, *that will do. I hope.*

我想是的。噢，我希望那件可以。

S : The balance will be NT$ 300.

相差台幣三百元。

C : O.K. Here you are.

好的，喏，拿去。

S : Thank you very much. 非常謝謝您。

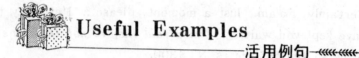

Useful Examples

活用例句

① *Do you have the receipt*?

① 您有收據嗎？

② We're very sorry *for the trouble* (*inconvenience*).

② 非常抱歉增加您的麻煩（不方便）。

③ Do you have *proof that* you bought it here?

③ 您能證明你是在這裏買的嗎？

④ *The balance* is NT$1,000.

④ 相差台幣一千元。

⑤ We're sorry to have troubled you.

⑤ 很抱歉造成您的麻煩。

⑥ We're sorry, we can't exchange *discount sale's goods*.

⑥ 抱歉，我們不換打折的商品。

⑦ We're sorry, we can't exchange *perishable goods*.

⑦ 抱歉，容易腐壞的物品我們不換。

⑧ We're sorry, we can't *refund your money*.

⑧ 很抱歉，我們不能退給您錢。

⑨ Because it is *a discount sale's* goods.

⑨ 因為它是打折商品。

⑩ Because it was used *improperly*.

⑩ 因為它被不正確的使用方法弄壞了。

⑪ *It will cost you more*. Will it be all right?

⑪ 它會使您花更多錢，可以嗎？

⑫ We would like to pay you back *in merchandise coupons*.

⑫ 我們想用商品優待券退給您。

⑬ May we pay you back in merchandise coupons?

⑬ 我們可以退給您商品優待券嗎？

⑭ We would like to *pay back the balance* in merchandise coupons.

⑭ 我們想要用商品優待券來補回差額。

⑮ *It is equivalent* to cash in our store.

⑮ 在我們店裏兌換現金是一樣的。

⑯ It is equivalent to cash *not only* in our store, *but* other department stores indicated here.

⑯ 不只在我們店裏可以兌現金，其他此地被指定的百貨店都可以。

【註】

exchange〔ɪksˈtʃendʒ〕*v.* 交換；掉換

treat〔trit〕*v.* 視爲

lingerie〔ˈlænʒə,ri〕*n.* 女用內衣（尤指品質較好之亞麻或絲製品）

all of a sudden 突然地　　crack〔kræk〕*n.* 裂縫

proof〔pruf〕*n.* 證據；證明　　receipt〔rɪˈsit〕*n.* 收據

trouble〔ˈtrʌbl̩〕*n.,v.* 麻煩；苦惱　*change one's mind* 改變心意

balance〔ˈbæləns〕*n.* 差額　　　　*fit (something) in* 裝配好；湊配

perishable〔ˈpɛrɪʃəbl̩〕*adj.* 易壞的　*n.pl.* 易壞之物

coupon〔ˈkupɑn〕*n.* 優待券；聯票

equivalent〔ɪˈkwɪvələnt〕*adj.* 相當的；相等的

indicate〔ˈɪndə,ket〕*v.* 指示；指出；象徵

It's covered by warranty.
修理的詢問

<会話実況>

　　顧客持電氣用品來店裏修理時，必須注意產品有無**保證書**及**保證期間的時效**，在修理前，也須說明費用，以免事後雙方發生爭執。如：*I'm sorry, there will be a charge because the warranty has expired.* 抱歉，這份保證書已經過期了，所以我們要收費的。

Dialogue 1

C : ***It's on the blink*** these days. ***Can you repair it***?
　　這幾天它壞了。你可以修理一下嗎？

S : Certainly, sir. Do you have ***the warranty certificate***?
　　當然可以，先生。您有沒有保證書？

C : Yes, I do. Here you are.
　　有。在這裏。

S : Thank you... All right. ***It's covered by warranty.***
　　謝謝您……好了。保證書已經抵償了費用。

C : You mean it's ***free of charge***?
　　你的意思是免費？

S : It certainly is. Would you please write your name, address, and phone number here?
　　當然。請您寫下您的大名、地址和電話。

C : Sure. How long will it take?
　　好的。要花多久能修好？

S : It will be ready in *a couple of* weeks. We will call you
when it's ready.

　　大概要幾個禮拜。修好時我們會打電話通知您。

C : I see. Thank you.

　　我明白了。謝謝你。

Dialogue 2

C : (*Showing a stub*) I've come to *pick up* my pants.

　　（現出存根）我來拿我的褲子。

S : Just a moment, please... Yes, they're here.

　　請稍等一下……對，它們在這兒。

C : How much does it cost?

　　需要多少錢？

S : Nothing. It's all *part of the service.*

　　不用了。這純粹是服務。

C : Oh, Thank you. 噢，謝謝。

Dialogue 3

C : Can you repair this?

　　你可以修理一下這個嗎？

S : *What's wrong with it*, ma'am?

　　出了什麼毛病，女士？

C : I don't know. But the sound doesn't come out of *the right
speaker.*

　　我不知道。但是右邊的喇叭似乎發不出聲音。

S : Oh, I see. 噢，我明白了。

C : I have the warranty certificate, so it's free of charge,
isn't it?

　　我有保證書，所以是免費服務，是不是這樣？

S : May I see it, please?... I'm sorry, but *the warranty has expired*, so I think there will be a charge.

　　請讓我看一下好嗎？……對不起，這份保證書已經過期了，所以我想還是要收費的。

C : Really? I can't read Chinese. Anyway, can you call me when it's ready?

　　眞的嗎？我看不懂中文。不過，修好時請你打電話通知我好嗎？

S : Certainly. Then, may I have your name, address, and phone number here on this slip?

　　當然。那麼請您在這張單子上寫上您的姓名、住址和電話號碼好嗎？

C : O.K.,... Here you go.

　　好的。……喏，寫好了。

S : Thank you, ma'am. It will be ready in 2 weeks.

　　謝謝您，女士。二星期之內會修理好。

C : Oh, no. *I can't wait that long.*

　　不行啊。我不能等那麼久。

S : We're really sorry. But *there's nothing we can do* about it. *This is how long it usually takes.*

　　眞的很抱歉。但是我們實在是沒辦法。一般都要這麼久的。

C : Are you sure?

　　你確定嗎？

S : Yes. 是的。

C : All right, then thank you.

　　好吧！那麼謝謝你。

S : Not at all. 不客氣。

Useful Examples
─────────────────活用例句→«««<«««

① Do you have *the warranty certificate*?

① 您有沒有帶保證書？

② *It's covered by warranty, so it's free of charge.*

② 保證書抵償了費用，所以費用全免。

③ I think there will be a charge because the warranty *has expired*.

③ 我想還是要收費，因為保證書已經過期了。

④ We can't *fix it free of charge* because it wasn't purchased here.

④ 我們無法免費修理它，因為它不是在這裏買的。

⑤ It's all *part of the service*, so it's free.

⑤ 它純粹是服務性質，所以是免費的。

⑥ I think it will be ready in two days.

⑥ 我想在兩天內會修好。

⑦ We'll call you when it's (they're) ready.

⑦ 它（們）修好時，我們會打電話通知您。

⑧ I think *it will be more economical* to buy a new one.

⑧ 我想，買一個新的會比較經濟些。

⑨ It's *on the blink*.

⑨ 它壞掉了。

⑩ *It is free of charge.*

⑩ 它是免費的。

⑪ We're sorry we can't *repair*
(*alter*, *mend*) it.

⑪ 很抱歉我們不能修。

⑫ Because the producer *is no
longer existent*.

⑫ 因爲製造商已經不存在
了。

⑬ Because it is not our merchandise.

⑬ 因爲這不是我們店裏賣
出的商品。

⑭ It would *be of no use* repairing
(altering, mending) this.

⑭ 修理這個是沒有用的。

⑮ It would be cheaper to buy a
new one.

⑮ 買個新的會比較省錢。

⑯ It is not necessary to repair
(alter, mend) it.

⑯ 沒有必要去修理它。

⑰ As it is *in good working
condition*.

⑰ 因爲它仍然完好無損。

⑱ As the short one is *in fashion*
this year.

⑱ 因爲今年流行短的。

⑲ *As it fits you well.*

⑲ 因爲它很適合您。

⑳ There is *a charge for the repair* (*alteration*, *work*), so
will it be all right?

⑳ 我們要收修理費用，可
以嗎？

㉑ It will be ready *by* four o'clock.

㉑ 我們四點鐘時會修好。

㉒ It will be ready *within* three
days.

㉒ 三天內會修好。

on the blink　〔俚〕壞的；需要修理的

repair〔rɪ'pɛr〕*v., n.* 修理

warranty certificate　保證書

cover〔'kʌvɚ〕*v.* 抵償；包括

warrant〔'wɑrənt〕*n.* 保證

certificate〔sɚ'tɪfəkɪt〕*n.* 證書

stub〔stʌb〕*n.* 存根；票根

speaker〔'spikɚ〕*n.* 擴音喇叭；說話者

expired〔ɪk'spaɪrd〕*adj.* 期滿；到期的

slip〔slɪp〕*n.* 單子；紙條

economical〔,ikə'nɑmɪkḷ〕*adj.* 經濟的；節省的

6 What does she look like?

廣播失物及小孩走失等

<會話實況>

在**人潮擁擠**的商店中，經常會發生遺失物品或小孩走丟的情況，
而此時正是考驗一個百貨服務層次最好的時機，所以在平時就應多
充實這方面的訓練。先問：*What does it*（*she*, *he*）*look like?*
它（她，他）是什麼樣子的？最後別忘了說，*It's all part of
our service.* 這純粹是為您服務。

Dialogue 1

C : I **lost** my bag. 我的袋子丟了。

S : Oh, I'm sorry. **What does it look like**?
噢，真替您難過。它是什麼樣子的？

C : It's black, **made of** leather, and has a shoulder strap.
黑的，皮製的，而且有條肩帶。

S : I see. We'll **check** it **out**, so just a moment, please... We
found it. We'll keep it at **the information desk** at the
main entrance.
我明白了。我們詢問一下，請稍待……找到了。我們將它保管在
大門的服務臺。

C : Oh, really? Thank you so much.
真的嗎？實在太謝謝你了。

S : Not at all. It's all part of the service. (*humorously*)
不客氣。這純粹是為您服務。（幽默地）

Dialogue 2

C : My daughter *is missing*.

我女兒走失了。

S : Oh, no. *What does she look like?*

噢，糟糕。她長得什麼樣子？

C : She's wearing a white blouse and a red skirt, and she has a small red bag.

她穿著白上衣，紅裙子，還帶一個紅色的小袋子。

S : I see. We'll check it out, so just a moment, please... *Here she is.*

我明白了。我們查詢一下，請您稍等一會……她在這兒。

C : Oh, thank you so much. (*To the girl*) Say 'Thank you'.

噢，真是太謝謝你了。(對著小女孩) 說謝謝。

G : Thank you. 謝謝。

S : You're welcome. 不客氣。

Dialogue 3

C : I think I *left* my wallet *behind* here, didn't I?

我想我把我的皮包丟在這兒了，有沒有？

S : Oh, just a moment, please. I'll check it out... *I'm afraid there is no such report.* Are you sure you left it here?

喔，請等一下。我問問看……恐怕沒有。您確定您是把它留在這兒嗎？

C : As far as I can remember.

我記得是這樣。

S : Then, we'll *search for* it throughout the store right away. Would you mind going to *the information desk* at the main entrance? We'll *take care of* it there.

那麼，我們馬上翻遍整個店為您找。您介意到大門服務臺嗎？我們
們會在那兒處理的。

C : Yes, thank you.
　　好的，謝謝你。

 Useful Examples
活用例句

① *What does it look like*?
　 What does he (she) look like?

① 它是什麼樣子？
　 他（她）長什麼樣子？

② *We'll check it out*, so just a
　 moment, please.

② 我們查詢一下，請稍待
　 片刻。

③ *I'm afraid* there's no such re-
　 port yet, but we'll *get* in
　 contact with you *as soon as*
　 we find it.

③ 恐怕還沒有消息，不過
　 我們一找到它就會馬上
　 跟您聯絡。

④ We'll *page* you as soon as we
　 find it.

④ 我們一找到它，就會立
　 刻喊您。

⑤ We found it (him, her).

⑤ 我們找到它（他，她）
　 了。

⑥ He (she) is now *at the infor-
　 mation desk at the main en-
　 trance*.

⑥ 他（她）現在在大門的
　 服務臺那兒。

⑦ We'll keep it at the toy
　 department.

⑦ 我們將它保管在玩具部
　 門。

⑧ *As far as I can remember*.

⑨ My daughter *is missing*.

⑩ *May I have your attention, please*? Paging Mr. Lewis from Tainan. Please report to the main entrance on the first floor. *Your companion is waiting for you there*. Thank you.

⑪ *Attention, please*. Paging our customer who just purchased a watch on the 6th floor. Please report back to the same department. *Your belongings were left behind there*. Thank you.

⑫ May I have your attention, please? Paging the mother of a lost child named Mary Smith. Please *report to* the information desk at the main entrance, on the first floor. She's waiting for you there. Thank you.

⑬ Will you please report it to our lost and found section?

⑭ I'm sorry to hear that.

⑧ 我記得是如此。

⑨ 我女兒不見了。

⑩ 請注意！台南來的路易士先生。請至一樓的大門口。您的同伴在那兒等您。謝謝。

⑪ 請注意！剛剛在六樓買錶的顧客。請您回到相同的部門。您的東西留在那裏。謝謝。

⑫ 請注意！有一位走失的小孩，名叫瑪莉‧史密斯,要找她的母親。請這位媽媽至一樓大門的服務臺。她在那兒等您，謝謝。

⑬ 請您到我們的失物招領部報到好嗎？

⑭ 我很遺憾。

⑮ Attention, please. Paging the mother of a lost girl about 3 years of age, who has a white blouse and a red skirt on. Please report to the information desk at the main entrance, on the first floor. She's waiting for you there. Thank you.

⑮ 請注意！有一個走失的三歲小女孩要找媽媽，小女孩穿著白上衣和紅裙子。請這位母親至一樓大門的詢問臺。她在那兒等您，謝謝。

⑯ May I have your attention, please? Paging Mr. Smith. *There is a telephone call for you*, so please *pick up the receiver at the nearest phone*. Thank you.

⑯ 請注意！史密斯先生。櫃台有您的電話，請至最近的電話接聽，謝謝。

⑰ We will let you know *as soon as it is reported*.

⑰ 只要它一被呈報出來，我們就會讓您知道。

⑱ We will give you a call if it is reported.

⑱ 一旦它報上來我們就會給您電話。

⑲ Can you describe it please?

⑲ 您能描述一下它嗎？

⑳ Can you give us *a description of* it?

⑳ 您能告訴我們它的特徵嗎？

㉑ Will you go to *our lost and found section*?

㉑ 請您到失物招領處好嗎？

㉒ May I have his (her) name?

㉒ 您能告訴我他（她）的名字嗎？

㉓ He（She）is now *at the infor-mation desk*.

㉓ 他（她）現在在服務臺。

㉔ Will you write down his（her）name here?

㉔ 請您在這裏寫下他（她）的名字好嗎？

㉕ How do you pronounce his（her）name?

㉕ 他（她）的名字要怎麼唸？

㉖ We are now calling him（her）.

㉖ 我們現在正在呼叫他（她）。

---

shoulder〔'ʃoldɚ〕*n.* 肩　　strap〔stræp〕*n.* 皮帶；帶

check out 查問　　information〔,ɪnfɚ'meʃən〕*n.* 詢問處；服務臺

humorously〔'hjumərəslɪ〕*adv.* 幽默地

missing〔'mɪsɪŋ〕*adj.* 失蹤的；不在的

blouse〔blauz〕*n.* 寬鬆的婦女或兒童之短衫

skirt〔skɝt〕*n.* 裙　　*leave behind* 忘記攜帶；遺落

wallet〔'wɑlɪt〕*n.* 皮包；皮夾　　*as far as* 就⋯所

search〔sɝtʃ〕*v.* 尋覓；搜索　　*take care of* 處理；照料

in contact with 聯繫

page〔pedʒ〕*v.*（在旅館、俱樂部中）喊出其名字以尋找（某人）

attention〔ə'tɛnʃən〕*n.* 注意；專心

belonging〔bɪ'lɔŋɪŋ〕*n.* 附屬物

receiver〔rɪ'sivɚ〕*n.* 聽筒；耳機

7 May I see your passport, please?

免稅品的處理

—< 會話實況 >—

用英文說明數字本來就頗繁複，而**免稅商品**（ *tax-free pur-chase* ）又牽涉更複雜的稅額計算，因此，對英文沒有把握的人，最好能在說了價錢之後，再用筆寫下來給顧客看，才不致發生誤解與糾紛。因為顧客會常問： *What's the tax rate?* 稅率是多少？

Dialogue 1

C : Does this price *include tax*?
　　這個價格有含稅嗎？

S : Yes, it does. *Any price above* $15,000 includes tax.
　　有的。任何高於一萬五千元的價格都有含稅。

C : I'll take it, and can you *make it tax-free*?
　　我要買這個，你可以免稅賣給我嗎？

S : *May I see your passport*, please?
　　請讓我看一下您的護照好嗎？

C : Oh, I don't have it with me now.
　　噢，我沒帶在身上。

S : I'm sorry, then we can't sell it to you tax-free.
　　那麼對不起，我們不能免稅賣給您。

C : O.K. I'll come back later with my passport.
　　好吧！我等會兒帶著護照再來。

S : Yes, please. 是的，請。

Dialogue 2

C : Can you ***make reductions on it for tax exemption***?

你可不可以扣除稅額，減個價呢？

S : Oh, this is not taxed to begin with. Those items cheaper than $15,000 are not taxed.

噢，這並沒有加稅。那些比一萬五千元便宜的項目都沒有加稅。

C : Oh, does that include $15,000?

噢，包括一萬五千元在內嗎？

S : Yes, ma′am. 是的，女士。

C : What′s the tax rate, by the way?

那麼稅率是多少？

S : It ***depends on*** the item, but for jewelry it′s 15%.

那要看是什麼項目，珠寶的話是百分之十五。

C : I see. 我明白了。

Dialogue 3

C : Can I have this tax-free?

我可以享受免稅的優待嗎？

S : May I see your passport, please?... I′m sorry, but ***it doesn′t qualify you for a tax-free purchase.*** You′re not a tourist, are you?

請讓我看一下您的護照好嗎？……很抱歉您並不符合購買免稅商品的條件。您不是個觀光客，是嗎？

C : You mean you can′t make a tax-free purchase if you′re not a tourist?

您的意思是，如果不是觀光客就不能購買免稅商品嗎？

S : Yes, that′s right.

是的，沒錯。

Dialogue 4

C : Can you make it tax-free?

　　它可以免税嗎？

S : May I see your passport, please?... Thank you. Just a
moment, please... It's $11,739, ma'am.

　　請讓我看一下您的護照，好嗎？謝謝。請等一下……女士，共一
　　萬一千七百三十九元。

C : Why do you *come up with* these small numbers? *What's the
tax rate*?

　　爲何有這些小數目呢？税率是多少？

S : The tax rate is 15%, but we can't subtract exactly 15%.

　　税率是百分之十五，但我們不能就正好將它的百分之十五扣除。

C : Why not?

　　爲何不？

S : Because it doesn't mean 15% of *the selling price* is tax.
The tax is 15% of *the original price. In other words*, the
selling price is 115% of the original price.

　　因爲這並不表示售價的百分之十五是税金。税金是原價的百分之
　　十五。換句話說，售價是原價的百分之一百一十五。

C : I see. Here you are.

　　我懂了。錢在這兒。

S : Thank you. Just a moment, please...

　　謝謝。請稍等……

Useful Examples
─────────────────活用例句─◀◀◀◀◀◀◀

① *May I see your passport, please*?

① 請讓我看一下護照，好嗎？

② I'm sorry, but *your passport doesn't qualify you for a tax-free purchase*. A tax-free purchase *is limited to* tourists.

② 對不起，您不能憑您的護照免稅購買物品。免稅購買物品者只限於觀光客。

③ The tax rate *depends on* the item.
The tax rate varies *from item to item*.

③ 稅率依物品而定。

各類物品之稅率有異。

④ We can't *subtract* 15% *from* the selling price.

④ 我們不能從售價中扣除百分之十五。

⑤ Those items below $10,000 *inclusively* are not taxed to *begin with*.

⑤ 那些價格低於一萬元的貨品未達可開始課稅的標準。

⑥ Can you make it tax-free?
Can I have it tax-free?
Can you make reductions on it for tax exemption?

⑥ 它可以免稅嗎？
我可以享免稅優待嗎？
你可以將它的稅金扣除以降低價格嗎？

⑦ Why do you *come up with* these small numbers?

⑦ 為何有這些小數目呢？

⑧ We're sorry, these are not tax-free items.

⑧ 很抱歉，這些不是免稅品。

⑨ We're sorry, *we don't handle any tax-free goods* at our store.

⑨ 很抱歉，我們店裏不賣免稅商品。

⑩ *How much would it be with tax exemption*?

⑩ 它扣除稅額後是多少錢?

⑪ It *depends on* the article.

⑪ 依物品類別而定。

⑫ The tax amount *differs* depending on the article.

⑫ 稅額依物品類別而有所不同。

⑬ The amount of tax is *from* ten *to* twenty percent depending on the items.

⑬ 稅額依照物品的類別不同而有百分之十到百分之二十的差別。

⑭ In this case, the tax amount is twelve percent.

⑭ 在這項上面，稅率是百分之十二。

⑮ *Will you fill out this form, please*?

⑮ 請您填好這張表格好嗎?

⑯ We will *fill in* the rest, sir (ma'am).

⑯ 先生（女士），我們會把其他部分填好。

⑰ May I have your signature, please?

⑰ 請您簽名好嗎?

⑱ It is 2,000 NT$ without the tax.

⑱ 不含稅是台幣兩千元。

⑲ Please *keep the receipt* (*card*), as you will need it *at customs*.

⑲ 請拿好收據（卡片），因為您在海關時會需要的。

⑳ We're sorry, you can't qualify for tax-free items.

⑳ 抱歉，您並不符合購買免稅品的條件。

㉑ We're sorry, you can't buy tax-free articles *on this passport*.

㉑ 很抱歉，您不能根據這個護照購買免稅商品。

㉒ *Only tourists can buy tax-free articles.*

㉒ 只有觀光客才能購買免稅品。

㉓ Only those tourists who have lived *less than three months* in Taiwan can buy tax-free items.

㉓ 只有在台灣居留期間不到三個月的觀光客，才能購買免稅商品。

㉔ We're sorry, these are not tax-free items.

㉔ 很抱歉，這些不是免稅品。

㉕ Tax-free articles *are limited to* cameras, watches and jewelry.

㉕ 免稅品限於照相機、手錶以及珠寶。

㉖ We're sorry, we don't *carry any tax-free items* here.

㉖ 很抱歉，在此我們不受理任何免稅商品。

㉗ *The tax amount* is very little, and our price *is almost the same as* that for tax-free items.

㉗ 稅額很小，所以我們的價格幾乎和免稅品沒什麼兩樣。

㉘ We have them on the fifth floor.

㉘ 我們在五樓經辦此事。

㉙ Our things are all at discount prices so that they are nearly the same as the tax-free prices.

㉙ 我們的東西都是打折過的價錢，所以幾乎和免稅品是一樣的價格。

tax-free〔'tæks'fri〕*adj.* 免稅的
passport〔'pæs,port〕*n.* 護照
reduction〔rɪ'dʌkʃən〕*n.* 減少；減低
exemption〔ɪg'zɛmpʃən〕*n.* 免除
item〔'aɪtəm〕*n.* 項目
jewelry〔'dʒuəlrɪ〕*n.* 珠寶之集合名稱
qualify〔'kwɑlə,faɪ〕*v.* 適合
tourist〔'tʊrɪst〕*n.* 觀光客；旅行者
come up with 追及；取出
subtract〔səb'trækt〕*v.* 扣除；減去
original〔ə'rɪdʒənl〕*adj.* 最初的；原來的
in other words 換句話說
vary〔'vɛrɪ〕*v.* 使不同；有變化
below〔bə'lo〕*prep.* 在…以下；不及
inclusively〔ɪn'klusɪvlɪ〕*adv.* 包含；包括一切
form〔fɔrm〕*n.* 表格；手續；形式
signature〔'sɪgnətʃɚ〕*n.* 簽字
customs〔'kʌstəmz〕*n.* 進口稅；海關

稅別專用術語

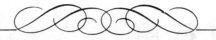

- *land value increment tax* 土地增值稅
- *stamp-duty* 印花稅（ = *stamp-tax* ）
- *business value-added tax* 加值稅（加值營業稅）
- *land value tax* 地價稅　　　　*homeowner's tax* 自宅稅
- *housing tax* 房屋稅　　　　　*property tax* 財產稅
- *protection tariff* 保護關稅
- *"special business" tax* 特種營業稅
- **taxpayer** 〔′tæks,peɚ 〕 *n.* 納稅人
- *obligation to pay tax* 納稅義務
- *national land tax* 國有土地稅
- *entertainment tax* 娛樂稅
- *alcohol & tobacco tax* 菸酒稅
- *slaughter tax* 屠宰稅　　　　*capital levy* 資本課稅
- *license tax* 牌照（執照）稅（ = *permit tax* ）
- *uniform income tax* 綜合所得稅
- *legacy tax* 遺產稅（ = *inheritance duty* ）
- **tariff** 〔′tærɪf 〕 *n.* 關稅（ = *customs duty* ）
- *import duty* 進口稅（ = *import tax* ）
- *transit tax* 轉口稅　　　　　**toll** 〔 tol 〕 *n.* 通行稅
- *tax receipt* 繳稅收據

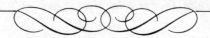

店員流行語

■ *What pieces would you like?* 您喜歡哪幾樣？

■ *I'm sorry we're all out.* 抱歉！全部賣完了。

■ *This line of ties just arrived from Hongkong yesterday.*
  這批領帶是昨天剛從香港運到的。

■ *Not at all.* 不客氣。

■ *Can I help you?* 您想要些什麼嗎？

■ *We sell many items.* 我們賣的種類很多。

■ *Shall I wrap this up as well as the other things?*
  這個和其他的那些東西都要包起來嗎？

■ *May I show them to you?* 要不要我都拿來給您看看？

■ *This price includes expressage.* 這個價錢包括運費在內。

■ *I'm just going window shopping.* 我祇是看看。

■ *Thank you for shopping with us. Good-bye.*
  謝謝惠顧，再見。

■ *They'll be delivered on Friday.* 星期五交貨。

■ *Good day.* 再見(白天告別時用語)　*Good night.* 再見(晚上告別時用語)

■ *By sea or air?* 海運還是空運呢？

■ *They sell exclusive goods at that store.*
  那家店專賣高級貨。

■ *That is a standing unit.* 那是站立型的。

■ *This kind is fully automatic.* 這種是全自動的。

■ *This pale green is very lovely.* 這種淡綠色很漂亮。

Part G

各式專櫃會話
VARIOUS DEPARTMENTS

What does E or double E mean?
鞋類專櫃

＜會話實況＞

顧客選購鞋類產品一定得試穿，有時甚至會碰到缺貨的情況，所以此類會話務必熟練活用。此外有一點必須特別注意的是，顧客**試鞋**時別忘了：*Would you like to have a seat*？請坐。

Dialogue 1

S：May I help you, sir？我可以為您效勞嗎，先生？

C：Do you have a size 42 in this style？
　　你們有沒有這種式樣42號的？

S：Just a moment, please. I'll **go and check our stock**…
　　I'm sorry to **have kept you waiting**. Please try these on.
　　請稍等一會，我去查查存貨……對不起讓您等這麼久。請試
　　看看。

C：Thanks…Umm…comfortable. How much is **this pair**？
　　謝謝……嗯……蠻舒適的。這一雙要多少錢？

S：It's ＄5,000, sir. 五千元，先生。

Dialogue 2

C：What does E or double E mean？
　　E或二個E是什麼意思？

S : They are to show how wide your shoes are. EE (*double E*) is wider than E, and EEE (*triple E*) is wider than EE (*double E*).

那是指您的鞋子多寬（大）。二個 E 比 E 寬（大）一點，而三個 E 比二個 E 更寬（大）一點。

C : Let me see... 我看看……

S : Would you like to **have a seat** ? 您想要坐下來嗎 ?

C : Oh, thank you. Do you have, then, double E of this style ? **They're too tight for me.**

噢，謝謝。你們有沒有這種式樣二個 E 寬（大）的 ? 這雙太緊了。

S : Just a moment, please... I'm sorry, but we've **run out of stock.** Would you like this style **instead** ?

請等一下……眞抱歉，正好缺貨。您要不要用這種式樣代替 ?

C : Umm... Not bad, but let me **think it over.** Thank you.

嗯……還不錯，但是讓我考慮一下。謝謝你。

S : You're welcome. Please come again.

不客氣，下次再來。

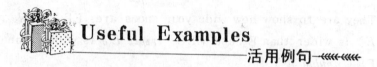

Useful Examples
活用例句

① Do you have a size 7½? 你們有7½號尺寸的鞋子嗎?

② I want two pairs of shoes *in this style*.
我要兩雙這種款式的鞋子。

③ Would you like to *have a seat*? 您要坐下嗎?(請坐。)

④ They're *too tight* for me. 這太緊了。

⑤ If you cannot go, *let him go instead*.
如果你不能去,讓他替你去。

⑥ Give me the red one *instead of* the green one.
給我紅色的,不要那綠色的。

⑦ Let me *go and check our stock*. 讓我去查查存貨。

⑧ How much does *this pair* cost? 這雙要多少錢?

⑨ Would you like to fit another pair on?
您想試穿別雙嗎?

⑩ We've *run out of* stock. 我們已經賣完了。

⑪ Please come again. 請再度光臨。

⑫ Couldn't you sell me one pair for $500?
你不能賣我一雙五百元嗎?

⑬ I *strongly recommend* this product. 我極力推薦這項產品。

⑭ Please let me *think it over*. 請讓我考慮考慮。

【註】

tight〔taɪt〕*adj.* 緊的　*run out of* 耗盡;用光
think over 仔細考慮　recommend〔͵rɛkə'mɛnd〕*v.* 介紹;推薦

鞋類專用術語

clog 〔klɑg；klɔg〕 *n.* 木屐

zori 〔'zorɪ〕 *n.* 日式拖鞋（＝ *Jap sandal*）

woolen bootee 毛線鞋（嬰兒）

halfboot 〔'hæf, but〕 *n.* 半長統靴

flat 〔flæt〕 *n.* 平跟鞋

oxford 〔'ɑksfəd〕 *n.* 用帶鞋（＝ *shoe with laces*）

leather shoe 皮鞋   *cloth shoe* 布鞋

loafer 〔'lofə〕 *n.* 包鞋   *canvas shoe* 帆布鞋

rainboot 〔'ren, but〕 *n.* 雨鞋（靴）（＝ *waterproof boot*）

toeshoe 〔'to, ʃu〕 *n.* 芭蕾舞鞋

walking shoe 便鞋

high heel 高跟鞋（＝ *high heeled shoe*）

sandal 〔'sændḷ〕 *n.* 涼鞋   *dress shoe* 晚宴鞋

sneaker 〔'snikə〕 *n.* 球鞋（＝ *sports shoe*；*gym shoe*）

spikes 〔spaɪks〕 *n.* 釘鞋（＝ *running shoe with spikes*）

ice skate 溜冰鞋（冰刀）   *roller skate* 溜冰鞋（輪子）

embroidered satin shoe 繡花鞋

basketball shoe 籃球鞋   *snow shoe* 雪鞋

slipper 〔'slɪpə〕 *n.* 拖鞋

riding boot 馬靴（＝ *high boot*）

I think
they are a little tight.
仕女服裝專櫃

─<會話實況>─

　　女孩子挑選服飾通常注意的層面甚廣，因此，店員必須熟知**花樣、款式、尺寸大小**(*pattern, design, size*)與品質、包裝等等許多細節，才能從容應付。只要她們滿意，日後一定經常光顧，信任這家的服務。

Dialogue 1

C : I bought one like this ***the day before yesterday***.
　　前天我買了一件和這件一樣的。

S : Oh, thank you very much. 噢，眞謝謝您。

C : But I ***left it behind*** at the hotel. I wanted something that can be worn underneath it. Do you recommend this plain one or one ***with the same pattern***?
　　但是我把它放在飯店裏。我想要一件可以穿在裏面的。你會推薦這件素色的還是這件相同花樣的？

S : I think I like this one better. (*She points at one with the same pattern.*)
　　我想我比較喜歡這件。(她指著那件相同花樣的。)

C : O.K. I′ll take it. 好吧！我買了。

S : Thank you very much. It′s $1,800. Is it a present?
　　眞謝謝您。一千八百元。這是個禮物嗎？

C : Yes, to my wife in America.

是的，送給我美國的太太。

S : Then, ***shall I put it in a box***?

那麼，要不要我用盒子裝起來？

C : No, just a bag is all right.

不用了，放在袋子裏就行了。

S : Certainly, sir.

好的，先生。

Dialogue 2

(*As a lady customer tries to **step into the fitting room** with her shoes on, an armful of swim suits in hand...*)

（有一個女顧客，抱著一堆游泳衣，腳上穿著鞋子，想要進入試穿間的時候…）

S : Excuse me, would you mind ***taking your shoes off***?

對不起，您介意脫掉您的鞋子嗎？

C : Oh, I'm sorry. 噢，對不起。

S : And I'm sorry, but you can't ***try on*** more than 2 items.

還是很抱歉，您最多祇能試穿二件。

C : Really? Then, this and this.

真的嗎？那麼就是這件和這件。

(*A few minutes later*) （幾分鐘之後）

S : How are you doing? 您覺得如何？

C : I think they are ***a little tight***. Do you have ***anything larger***?

我覺得有點緊。你們有沒有大一點的？

S : No, we don't. ***It's the largest size we have***.

沒有了。這是我們有的最大尺寸。

C : O.K. I'll take them. 好吧。我買了。

S : Thank you very much. We'd appreciate it very much if you
could **bear in mind** that because of the nature of the
merchandise, we can **neither** exchange your purchase **nor** give
you a refund.

真是謝謝您。如果您能把一件事牢記在心的話，我們會非常感謝您，
因為為了確保產品的品質，我們無法讓您交換或退還您購買的物品。

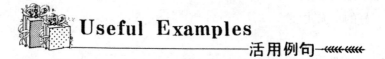 # Useful Examples
————————————————活用例句-◀◀◀◀◀◀◀◀

① I want to buy one miniskirt like this.
我想買一件和這一件一樣的迷你裙。

② You're quite right. 您說得很對。

③ **That's a good idea.** 好主意。

④ **What did you think of** our store?
您覺得我們的店怎麼樣？

⑤ I'm sure **you'll be pleased with this.**
我有把握您對這東西一定會滿意。

⑥ **Let me ask for permission first.** 我得先徵求同意。

⑦ Could you explain more specifically?
您能不能說得再明確一點？

⑧ **Excuse me for speaking in Chinese.**
對不起，我用中文說。

⑨ **Will you excuse me?** 失陪了。

⑩ Shall I put it in a box? 要不要我用盒子裝起來？

【註】————————◆◆

underneath〔ˌʌndəˈniθ〕*prep.* 在…之下

recommend〔ˌrɛkəˈmɛnd〕*v.* 介紹；推薦

plain〔plen〕*adj.* 樸素的；無裝飾的　　armful〔ˈɑrmˌfʊl〕*n.* 一抱之量

swim suit 泳衣　　item〔ˈaɪtəm〕*n.* 項目

appreciate〔əˈpriʃɪˌet〕*v.* 感激；重視　　*bear in mind* 牢記在心

permission〔pəˈmɪʃən〕*n.* 許可；准許　　nature〔ˈnetʃə〕*n.* 性質；品質

merchandise〔ˈmɝtʃənˌdaɪz〕*n.* 商品

refund〔rɪˈfʌnd〕*v.* 退還

女裝專用術語

- **monokini**〔͵mɑnə'kini〕*n.* 一件頭的比基尼泳衣
- **basque**〔bæsk〕*n.* 一種女用短上衣
- *V-neck blouse* V領罩衫
- *tank top* 女人之寬鬆上衣〔美〕
- **underwear**〔'ʌndə͵wɛr〕*n.* 女內衣(= *underclothes, lingerie*)
- **gown**〔gaʊn〕*n.* 女用長禮服　　**dress**〔drɛs〕*n.* 女用洋裝
- *low-cut dress* 女低胸衣　　*long dress* 女長衣
- *maternity clothes* 女性孕裝
- *girls' dress* 女童裝
- **jersey**〔'dʒɝzɪ〕*n.* 女衞生衫
- **blouse**〔blaʊz; blaʊs〕*n.* 女襯衫
- **bikini**〔bɪ'kinɪ〕*n.* 比基尼泳裝
- *little-girl style clothes* 娃娃裝
- *midi dress* 迷地裝
- *three-piece suit*(*skirt, vest, jacket*)套裝(連裙三件)
- **extravaganza**〔ɪk͵strævə'gænzə, ɛk-〕*n.* 強調女性美的春裝
- *evening dress* 晚禮服　　　　*bridal veil* 新娘披紗
- *bridal gown* 新娘禮服(= *bridal gown, wedding dress*)
- *ch'i p'ao* 旗袍

3 Can you select one for me that goes well with this suit?

領帶專櫃

<＜會話實況＞>

　　領帶是**搭配**男士正式服裝不可缺少的點綴，因此它並不能單獨選用，而必須搭配西裝外套或襯衫的顏色、款式，所以顧客常會要求店員：*Can you select one for me that goes well with this suit*？你可以替我選一條能搭配這套衣服的領帶嗎？

Dialogue 1

S : May I help you, sir？我能為您效勞嗎？先生？

C : ***Does it have a reduced price*** ？它有沒有減價？

S : Yes, that's right. We offer them ***at half price*** .
　　　有的。我們打五折。

C : Are they only for summer use？他們祇能在夏天用嗎？

S : No, ***they are made of*** 100% ***silk***, so it doesn't matter.
　　　You can wear it in any season.
　　　不，他們是百分之百純絲製成的，所以不受影響。
　　　您可以在任何季節戴它。

C : Can you select one for me ***that goes well with*** this suit？
　　　你可以替我選一條來配這套西裝嗎？

S : Yes, certainly, sir. I think the wine tinge is better. How
　　　would you like this one？
　　　當然，先生。我認為淡酒紅色比較好。您覺得這條如何？

C：Hmm…Nice. O.K., I'll take it. How much is it？

　　嗯…不錯。好，我買這條。多少錢？

S：It's $800, $800 out of $1,000. Just a moment, please...
I'm sorry too have kept you waiting. *Here's your change.*
That's $200. *Please double-check it.*

　　八百元。收您一千元，請稍等一下……

　　很抱歉讓您久等了。這是您的零錢，找您二百元。

　　請仔細清點一下。

C：Thank you. 謝謝。

S：Thank you. Have a nice day and please come again.

　　謝謝您。祝您有愉快的一天並請再度光臨。

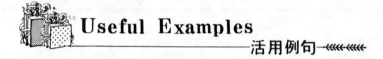

Useful Examples
活用例句

① We offer them *at half price*. 我們打五折。

② Sure, I'll get them for you. 好的，我拿給你。

③ We can only do（*undertake*）*simple mending.*

　　我們只受理簡單的縫補。

④ *What kind of stain* is it, sir.？

　　是哪一種污點呢？

⑤ *Have a nice day.* 祝您有愉快的一天。

⑥ That's O.K. *It's not urgent.*

　　沒關係，並不急著要。

⑦ Sure. *I'll do that.*

　　當然，我會照辦。

silk〔sɪlk〕*n.* 絲綢

select〔sə'lɛkt〕*v.* 挑選

go well with 相配

tinge〔tɪndʒ〕*n.* 微染；輕淡的顏色

double-check〔'dʌbḷ't∫ɛk〕*v.* 仔細檢查

mend〔mɛnd〕*v.* 修補；改正

stain〔sten〕*n.* 污點；染料

urgent〔'ɝdʒənt〕*adj.* 緊急的；急迫的

4 Is it genuine pearl?

寶石專櫃

<會話實況>

　　珠寶的璀璨稀有，人人皆愛，但它因色澤、品質及大小而有價位上的區別，並非人人皆買得起，所以在選購寶石時，除了要能區分真假之外，還須能鑑賞其 *color* 顏色，*clarity* 清澈度，*cut* 磨度，*carat* 重量，*crystal* 晶度，*culture* 養殖度。

Dialogue 1

C : *Is it genuine pearl*? 它是真的珍珠嗎？

S : Yes. Cultured pearl means it's genuine.
　　是的。養珠就表示它是真的。

C : What *makes the difference* in price?
　　在價格上如何區分呢？

S : *It depends on the quality and size.* Pearls of higher quality have better gloss.
　　要視品質與大小而定。高品質的珍珠色澤較好。

C : I see... Do you have a 16-inch in this type?
　　我懂了…你們有沒有這種式樣十六吋的？

S : Yes, certainly. It's over here. 當然有。在這裏。

C : I'll take it. But *is it possible to make knots in-between each pearl*?
　　我買了。但是有沒有可能在每一個珍珠之間打個結呢？

S : Sure, but it will take about 20 to 30 minutes. Would that
be all right？

可以，但是要花二十至三十分鐘的時間。可以嗎？

C : Yes, I'll look around the store and *come back later.*

好的，我會在附近逛逛，等會兒再來。

S : Certainly. How many knots each would you like？

好的。您希望在每個珍珠當中打幾個結？

C : Just one is enough. 一個就夠了。

S : All right. *We'll be waiting for you.*

好的。我們會在這裏等您。

C : Thank you. 謝謝。

S : Thank you. 謝謝您。

 Useful Examples
───────── 活用例句 ◄◄◄◄◄◄

① *Is it genuine jade*？ 它是真的玉嗎？

② *What makes the difference in price*？

價格上的差別是如何造成的呢？

③ I'll send someone immediately. 我立刻派人過去。

④ *What are your rates*？ 怎麼收費呢？

⑤ I'd like to use a *safety deposit box.*

我想使用保險櫃。

⑥ I see, sir. Could you *fill out* this form, please？

我知道了，先生。請填寫這張表格好嗎？

⑦ Could you *leave any valuables with* the front Cashier,

please？ 請把貴重物品寄放在出納處好嗎？

【註】━━━━━━━━━━━━━━━━◆◆

genuine〔ˈdʒɛnjʊɪn〕*adj.* 眞正的　　gloss〔glɔs〕*n.* 光澤

cultured〔ˈkʌltʃəd〕*adj.* 養殖的　　knot〔nɑt〕*n.* 結　*v.* 打結

jade〔dʒed〕*n.* 　翡翠；玉　　***safety deposit box*** 保險櫃

fill out 填妥　　valuable〔ˈvæljʊəbl̩〕*n.* 貴重物品；珠寶

舉一反三

C : I'm looking for a pearl necklace.

　　我想要一串珍珠項鍊。

S : Is it for you? 是您自己要的嗎？

C : No, it's for my wife. It's our anniversary.

　　不是的，是要送給我太太的結婚周年紀念。

S : Oh, congratulations. 噢，恭喜您。

C : Thanks, show me what you've got.

　　謝謝，給我看看你們的東西吧！

S : O.K., how do these look? 好的，這些怎麼樣？

C : I like this set here. 我喜歡這邊這組。

S : Ah, this one is our best. You have a fine eye for pearls.

　　啊，這是最好的。您鑑賞珍珠的眼光眞行。

C : How much is it? 多少錢？

S : This set is $30,000. 這組是三萬元。

C : Here you are. 拿去吧！

S : Thank you, and have a happy anniversary.

　　謝謝您，祝您結婚周年快樂。

珠寶專用術語

- *single strand of beads*　一串珠
- *matching set of jewels*　一套首飾
- *simulated pearl*　人造珍珠
- *synthetic*（*man-made*）*gem*（*stone*）　人造寶石
- *costume jewelry*　人造寶飾
- *simulated*（*synthetic*, *imitation*）*diamond*　人造鑽石
- trinket〔'trɪŋkɪt〕*n.* 小飾物（= *charm*）
- locket〔'lɑkɪt〕*n.* 小懸盒（掛於項鍊下）（= *pendant*）
- crystal〔'krɪstḷ〕*n.* 水晶
- bangle〔'bæŋgḷ〕*n.* 手鐲；環飾（= *bracelet*）
- jade（ite）〔dʒed〕*n.*（硬）玉
- platinum〔'plætnəm〕*n.* 白金
- *be gold filled*　包金
- alloy〔ə'lɔɪ, 'ælɔɪ〕*n.* 合金
- earring〔'ɪr,rɪŋ〕*n.* 耳環
- ring〔rɪŋ〕*n.* 戒指
- shell〔ʃɛl〕*n.* 貝殼
- beads〔bidz〕*n.* 念珠　　　*gold leaf*　金葉
- *gold*（*silver*）*bullion*　金（銀）塊

珠寶專用術語

- *gold chain* 金鍊
- **sardonyx** 〔 ˊsɑrdənɪks 〕 *n.* 紅（紋）瑪瑙
- **ruby** 〔 ˊrubɪ 〕 *n.* 紅寶石
- **zircon** 〔 ˊzɝkɑn 〕 *n.* 風信子玉；鋯石
- **pearl** 〔 pɝl 〕 *n.* 珍珠
- **coral** 〔 ˊkɑrəl 〕 *n.* 珊瑚；海花石
- **corundum** 〔 kəˊrʌndəm 〕 *n.* 剛石
- *sterling silver* 純銀
- **ivory** 〔 ˊaɪvərɪ 〕 *n.* 象牙
- **topaz** 〔 ˊtopæz 〕 *n.* 黃玉（晶）
- *priceless treasure* 無價之寶
- **amber** 〔 ˊæmbɚ 〕 *n.* 琥珀　　**enamel** 〔 ɪˊnæml̩ 〕 *n.* 琺瑯
- **touchstone** 〔 ˊtʌtʃˌston 〕 *n.* 試金石（ = *lydian stone* ）
- **heirloom** 〔 ˊɛrˌlum 〕 *n.* 傳家寶
- **emerald** 〔 ˊɛmərəld 〕 *n.* 綠寶石；翡翠
- **agate** 〔 ˊægət 〕 *n.* 瑪瑙
- *cultured pearl* 養珠
- **cat's-eye** 〔 ˊkætsˌaɪ 〕 *n.* 貓眼（寶）石
- **sapphire** 〔 ˊsæfaɪr 〕 *n.* 藍寶石；青玉

5 It's not made in that pattern.
西式瓷器專櫃

Dialogue 1

C : Do you have *a sugar pot with the same pattern* as these tea cups? 你們有沒有和這些茶杯相同圖案的糖罐？

S : I'm sorry, but it's not made in that pattern. We have *some other series* over here.

很抱歉，沒有那種圖案的。但這裡有其他的系列。

Dialogue 2

C : Do you have something like this ?

(*She holds out a photo* .)

你們有沒有像這樣的東西？（她拿出一張照片。）

S : Just a moment, please. *I'll go and check it out* ... I'm sorry, but they are *only for export* and not for sale in Taiwan. But *I think they can be obtained to order* . I'll go and *inquire of* the producer, so would you please give me some more time? ... They say they have some *in stock*, so we can have them the day after tomorrow.

請稍等一下，我去問問看……很抱歉，他們專供外銷，在台灣是不賣的。但是我想可以用訂購的。我去問一下製造商，所以請您再給我一點時間好嗎？……他們說他們有一些存貨，所以我們後天可以拿到。

C : Then will you deliver them to my hotel? I'll be back from Taipei in *4* days.

那麼請你送到我的飯店好嗎？我再過四天就要從台北回去了。

S : Certainly, ma'am. Would you please write your name, and the name and room number of your hotel here?

是的，女士。請您在這兒寫上您的姓名及飯店名稱和房間號碼，好嗎？

C : *What if they don't reach me*?

如果他們沒聯絡到我怎麼辦？

S : Please call us at this number. My name is Jane.

請您打這支電話給我們。我的名字是珍。

C : All right. 好吧。

S : *We'd like you to pay now*, *please*. It's $2,800, ma'am.

請您先付帳，二千八百元，女士。

Dialogue 3

C : I want *180* of these glasses, but *I'm not sure how much tax will be imposed*. Can you calculate it?

我要這一百八十個玻璃杯，但我不知道要加多少稅。你能算出來嗎？

S : They are tax-free, but they'll probably be taxed at the customs when you get back to your country. I'm sorry we don't know *how to figure it out.*

他們是免稅的，但也許在您回去您的國家時，在海關會課稅。對不起，我不知道怎麼算。

C : Can you make some reductions?

你能不能算便宜一點？

S : Just a moment, please. (*He talks it over with her boss.*) *.... Our best offer is 15 % off.*

請等一下。（他和老闆討論了一下。）⋯⋯最多祇能打八五折。

C : How much will it cost *for overseas shipping*?

如果用海運寄到國外要多少錢？

S : *Would you mind waiting a little longer*? I'll check it out... I'm very sorry to have kept you waiting. Transportation, packing, and insurance come to $5,500.

請您再等一會兒，我去查查看⋯⋯抱歉讓您久等了。連運費、包裝費和保險費總共是五千五百元。

C : O.K. Let me think it over. Thank you.

好的，讓我考慮考慮。謝謝你。

S : You're welcome. Please come again. 不客氣。下次再來。

Dialogue 4

C : Is this made of *100 %* silver? 這是百分之百純銀做的嗎？

S : *That's silver-plated*, ma'am. 那是鍍銀的，女士。

C : Is it washable? 可以洗嗎？

S : Yes, but it turns black *little by little*. There's a polish available, so you can shine it up. 可以，但是會愈變愈黑。有一種有效的銀器粉，你可以用來擦亮它。

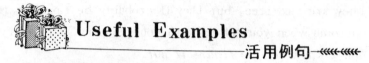

Useful Examples
活用例句

① Do you have any of these *credit cards*?

您有沒有這些公司的信用卡？

② *How would you like to settle your bill*?

您打算如何付款？

③ Do you have any other *documents*? 您還有其他證件嗎？

④ Now I'll *make out a receipt* and you can take it to Mr. Jones. 我現在開一張收據，請你拿給瓊斯先生。

⑤ This one is rare and difficult *to come by* (*get possession of*). 這東西很稀有，且難到手。

⑥ Let me assure you that we will always *give you our best service*. 我保證我們會給您最好的服務。

⑦ Yes, *I'm quite a stranger.*

是的，我在此人地生疏。

【註】

pot〔pɑt〕 *n.* 罐；壺   obtain〔əb'ten〕 *v.* 獲得
document〔'dɑkjəmɛnt〕 *n.* 證件   *make out a receipt* 開收據
possession〔pə'zɛʃən〕 *n.* 持有；所有權
stranger〔'strendʒɚ〕 *n.* 陌生人；異鄉人；外國人
impose〔ɪm'poz〕 *v.* 課（稅）   calculate〔'kælkjə,let〕 *v.* 計算；估計
custom〔'kʌstəm〕 *n.* 進口稅   *overseas shipping* 海運
transportation〔,trænspɚ'teʃən〕 *n.* 運送
insurance〔ɪn'ʃʊrəns〕 *n.* 保險金額
silver-plated〔'sɪlvɚ'pletɪd〕 *adj.* 鍍銀的；包銀的
washable〔'wɑʃəbḷ〕 *adj.* 可洗的
polish〔'pɑlɪʃ〕 *v.* 磨光擦亮   *n.* 光澤；擦銀器粉

How about coasters or vases?
日式瓷器專櫃

─＜會話實況＞─

　　日式瓷器通常較中國化，著重**實用性**，因此大都製成家用器皿，如 *coasters*（茶杯墊），*vases*（花瓶），*bowls*（碗），*dish*（碟），*plate*（盤），*cup*（杯），*saucer*（小杯碟）。

Dialogue 1

S : Good morning, ma'am. May I help you?
　　早安，女士。我可以為您效勞嗎？

C : Can you help me find something *for a souvenir*?
　　你能幫我選一樣紀念品嗎？

S : Certainly. I think *it's better to save space*, so how about coasters or vases? They are both painted with genuine japan. 當然可以。我想最好是不佔空間的，所以茶杯墊或是花瓶如何？他們都塗有真漆。

C : Genuine japan? What's that? 真漆？那是什麼？

S : It's a kind of lacquer paint. It's *made from* the sap of japan trees. It's a little expensive *compared to* other ones, *because those trees are becoming few and far between.* 是一種漆器上的畫。是用漆樹的樹液做成的。和別的比起來有點貴，因為那些樹愈來愈少而且間隔很遠。

C : Then I'll take two of these vases. 那麼我要買這兩個花瓶。

S : Certainly. It's $5,000 a piece, so $10,000 altogether.
好的。一個五千元，所以總共是一萬元。

C : Can I use this card? 我可以用信用卡嗎？

S : Yes, certainly. May I have your signature here, please? ...
Thank you. Just a moment, please... *Here's your card and
copy, and this is your purchase.*
當然。請您在這簽名好嗎？……謝謝您。請稍等一下……這是您
的卡及影印本，還有您買的東西。

C : Can I use them *in the same way as* ordinary dishes?
我可以和一般器皿一樣的使用他們嗎？

S : The instructions are given inside, but please be careful
not to *soak them in water* for a long time.
裡面附有說明書，但要小心不要把他們泡在水裡太久。

C : I see. Thank you for everything.
我明白了。這一切真謝謝你。

S : Thank you. *Have a nice trip.* 謝謝。祝您有個愉快的旅行。

Dialogue 2

S : May I help you, ma'am? 我可以為您效勞嗎，夫人？

C : How much are these plates? 這些盤子要多少錢？

S : The biggest one is $*1,000*, the medium one $*800*, and
the smallest, $*600*.
大的要 *1,000* 元，中的要 *800* 元，小的要 *600* 元。

C : I want six each of the $*1,000* and $*600* ones, and six of
the cup-and-saucer.
我要 *1,000* 元的和 *600* 元的各六個，還要六個杯碟。

S : I'm very sorry, *but we sell them in sets of five*, which
are $*1,400*, but we can't sell six of them at a time.

很抱歉，我們是以一組五個，售價一千四百元賣出的，所以沒辦法一次賣六個。

C : Oh, then,... I'll take *2* sets. And I want you to send them over to the States. How much will it cost?

噢，那麼，……我買二組。而且我希望你能寄到美國。這樣要多少錢？

S : I'll go and check it out, so would you mind waiting for a minute? ... I'm sorry to have kept you waiting. Airmail takes about a week and costs about $*10,000*, and sea mail takes about a month and a half and costs $*6,000*.

我去查一查，所以請您等一會兒好嗎？……眞對不起讓您久等。空運需要一個星期左右，費用大約是一萬元，而海運大約要一個半月，費用是六千元。

C : Then *I'll take the airmail*. How much do I owe you now?

那麼我要用空運的。這樣我總共要給你多少？

S : We only *accept your payment for your purchase* here. The shipping charge will be handled at the Overseas Shipping Department. I'll show you there anyway.

我們這裡只收取您購物所付的款項，至於運費則必須到海外運輸部門去辦理，不過我會告訴您在哪裡。

C : O.K. 好的。

S : Then it's $*12,400*, please. 那麼總共是一萬二千四百元。

C : I want to use my card. 我想用信用卡。

S : Certainly... *May I have your signature here please*? .... Thank you. This is your copy. I will take you to the Overseas Shipping Department now...(*At the department*).

He will take care of you. Please come again. 當然可以……

請您在此簽名好嗎？……謝謝您。這是影印本。現在我帶您到海外運輸部門……（ 在部門 ）他會照料您，請下次再來。

C : Thank you. 謝謝您。

Useful Examples
活用例句

① She *takes care of* a ten-room house without help.

　她獨力管理有十個房間的房子。

② Then *you are a non-resident, sir*?

　那麼，您是一個非住民，對嗎，先生？

③ Pardon? 請再說一遍？

④ I beg your pardon. 請再說一次。

⑤ Well, it is rather a large amount.

　嗯，這是一筆相當大的數目。

⑥ *Will* we *be seeing* you often? 我們以後能常常見到您嗎？

⑦ I have a *message* to deliver to you. 我有話要拜託你轉告。

⑧ I am looking for something *for a souvenir*.

　我在找些紀念品。

⑨ Here's your change. 這是找您的零錢。

⑩ *Have a nice trip.* 祝您有個愉快的旅行。

【註】

japan〔dʒəˈpæn〕*n.* 漆（器）

coaster〔ˈkostɚ〕*n.* 茶杯墊；置玻璃杯或花瓶之小盤子

lacquer〔ˈlækɚ〕*n.* 漆器　　　sap〔sæp〕*n.* 樹液

signature〔ˈsɪɡnətʃɚ〕*n.* 簽字　　soak〔sok〕*v.* 浸泡

medium〔ˈmidɪəm〕*adj.* 中等的　　saucer〔ˈsɔsɚ〕*n.* 小碟

handle〔ˈhændḷ〕*v.* 應付；管理

7 My friend wants to buy a doll whose head is made of porcelain.
洋娃娃專櫃

<會話實況>

　　洋娃娃是每一個女孩子童年時最**美麗**的夢想，很多成人仍然喜歡選購洋娃娃，是因為洋娃娃的造型總是推陳出新，漂亮可愛，至於材質總有千百種，所以店員必須知道如何回答：*It is made of plastics.* 它是用塑膠做的。

Dialogue 1

C : A friend of mine wants me to buy a doll whose head *is made of* porcelain. Is this porcelain?

　　我的一個朋友要我買一個頭是瓷做的娃娃。這是瓷器嗎？

S : No, sir. That's what is called PURAGASHIRA which means it's made of plastic, and this one over here is what is called HONGASHIRA. It's made of sawdust. It sounds cheap, but it's of high-class quality.

　　不是，先生。那是所謂的塑膠頭，意思是塑膠製的，而在這邊的這個叫做木屑頭，是鋸屑製成的。聽起來蠻便宜的，但它是高品質。

C : Well **they don't look different to me.**

　　嗯，他們對我來說看起來沒什麼兩樣。

S : They look alike because they are painted the same way.

　　他們看起來很像，因為是用同樣的手法畫的。

C : Let me see....O.K., Then I'll take this one with a fan.

讓我想想…。好吧，那麼我買這個有扇子的。

S : Thank you. 謝謝您。

Dialogue 2

C : Can you send this doll to the United States?

你可以把這娃娃寄到美國去嗎？

S : Yes, certainly. 當然可以。

C : *How long will it take*? 要花多久的時間？

S : *It depends on how you send it*. Would you like it by air or sea? Airmail takes about a week, but sea mail takes about 40 days.

要看您要怎麼寄。您想要空運還是海運？空運大概要一星期，而海運則需要40天左右。

C : Then I'll take the airmail. 那麼我要用空運的。

S : The charge will be about $3,600.

運費是三千六百元。

C : That much? 那麼多啊？

S : Yes, it's *twice as much as* the sea mail.

是的，是海運的兩倍。

C : Umm.... I think *I'll change my mind*. I'll take the sea mail. *By the way*, can you send its case, too?

嗯…我想我要改變主意了。我要用海運的。對了，可否連它的盒子一起寄？

S : Of course. 當然。

C : Is it ever possible that it might break?

有沒有可能會破掉？

S : No. We disassemble them first, and then pack them separately, so ***there's no need to worry about it***. Even if it
did break, ***it would all be covered by insurance***.

不會的。首先，我們會將它們解體，然後分開包裝，所以不需要
去擔心。即使它眞的破了，也都列入保險之中了。

C : I see, then I want both of them sent over.

我懂了，那麼我要它們兩個一起寄過去。

S : Just a moment, please. I'll go and pack them up. We
accept your payment for your purchase here, but would you
please go over to the Overseas Shipping Department on the
6th floor ***for other procedures*** as well as the shipping
charge?

請稍等一下，我去把它們包裝起來。我們這裏祇接受您購物的款
項，請您到六樓的海外運輸部門辦理其他手續，包括運費的付款。

C : ***What about*** my doll? Do I have to take it there with me?

我的娃娃怎麼辦？我需要把它帶到那兒嗎？

S : Yes, please.

是的。

C : All right. How much do I owe you here?

好吧。在這兒我需要付多少？

S : That'll be $8,800, sir.

八千八百元，先生。

Useful Examples
──活用例句──

① They don't look different to me.

　它們對我而言，並沒兩樣。

② *How long will it take*？ 要花多久時間？

③ It's *twice as much as* the sea mail. 它是海運的兩倍。

④ I *change my mind*. 我改變主意了。

⑤ It would be covered by insurance.

　它都列入保險之中了。

⑥ Do you have a reservation with us, sir？

　先生，您向本店預約過嗎？

⑦ By credit card. 用信用卡。

⑧ *It depends*. 視情形而定。

⑨ The clerk said that this is the best-selling product.

　店員說這項產品最暢銷。

⑩ *This is selling very well* in Taiwan.

　這樣東西在台灣很暢銷。

⑪ It's not expensive, *considering its quality*.

　以這種品質，賣這種價錢不算貴。

⑫ Let's *take a look at* some other stores if you have the time.

　如果有時間的話，我們多看幾家。

⑬ I know a store *that is offering a better price*.

　我知道有家店售價更低。

⑭ Let me *negotiate with* the clerk and try to get more
discount. 我跟店員講價，讓他多打點折扣。

⑮ I hope you enjoyed the day. 希望您今天玩得很愉快。

porcelain〔'porslɪn〕*n.* 瓷

sawdust〔'sɔ,dʌst〕*n.* 鋸屑

fan〔fæn〕*n.* 扇子；風扇

by the way 順便說

disassemble〔,dɪsə'sɛmbl̩〕*v.* 拆開；解離

procedure〔prə'sidʒɚ〕*n.* 手續；程序

reservation〔,rɛzɚ'veʃən〕*n.* 預定；保留

consider〔kən'sɪdɚ〕*v.* 視為；顧及；思考

negotiate〔nɪ'goʃɪ,et〕*v.* 商議

This is battery-powered.
玩具專櫃

<會話實況>

　　玩具部門總是充滿了新奇有趣的產品及小孩子要求父母購買的吵鬧聲，通常**父母幫孩子選購玩具**時，除了要注意玩具的購造及是否能激發孩子的想像力之外，最重要的是它的**安全性**，通常店員都會說：*It is battery-powered, so I'll try it out for.* 這是使用電池的，我試給您看。

Dialogue 1

C : Excuse me. Can you show me this？

　　對不起，你拿這個給我看一下，好嗎？

S : Certainly.... This one？　好的… 。這個嗎？

C : Yes. 是的 。

S : This is **battery-powered**, so I′ll **try** it **out** for you... We have a couple of levers over here, and if you lean the left one forward, *it moves forward*. If you lean it to the back, it moves backward. And the right one controls the sideways movement. *Right to the right, and left to the left*.

　　這是電池動力的，所以我試給您看… 。這兒有一對手桿，如果您把左手邊的傾向前，它會向前動。如果您傾向後，它會向後。而右邊的則是控制左右的移動。向右傾就會向右，向左傾就會向左。

C : I see. What kind of batteries does it use？

　　我懂了。它使用的是什麼電池？

S : You need one of this kind（006p）for the transmitter and another two for *the receiver*, and four of this type（SUM-2）for *the driving function itself*.

您需要一個這種的（006p）給發射器，還要另外二個給接收器，而要四個這種型式的（SUM-2）作為它自己的發動作用。

C : Can I get them in the States？

我在美國買得到這些電池嗎？

S : Yes, *it's a universal standard throughout the world*.

可以，它是全世界通行的一般標準。

C : Then, it's okay. I want my bags *as* light *as possible*.

那樣就好。我希望我的袋子愈輕愈好。

S : You can also use what is called NiCad batteries.

您也可以使用這種所謂的充電電池。

C : What are they？ 他們是什麼？

S : NiCad batteries. It's short for nickel and cadmium.

充電電池。它缺少了鎳和鎘兩種元素。

C : What does that mean？ 那表示什麼？

S : It's battery that you can *recharge over and over*, say, about 300 times. But you can't get them in the States.

那是一種您可以重覆地充電約三百次的電池。但是您在美國買不到。

C : I see. 我明白了。

S : This car over here already has a charger, so you don't have to *take* the batteries *out of* the car when you charge them. But this one doesn't have a charger inside, so *it's a little bothersome*. Of course, we have a separate charger available.

這部車本身有個充電器，所以當您要充電時，不需要把裏面的電池拿出來。但另外這輛並沒有充電器在裏面，所以就有點麻煩。當然，我們有個別的充電器可以用。

C : About how many hours does it take to *charge* them *up*?

大概要多久的時間才能把電充滿？

S : About 14 hours. Please be careful not to overcharge them. *It will kill the batteries faster.*

大約十四小時。請小心不要充電過量。那會使電池的壽命減短。

C : I see.... O.K. I'll change my mind and take the one with the charger inside and those batteries, as many as I need. Four, right?

我懂了…。好吧，我改變主意要買這輛有充電器的，還有這些我需要的電池。四個，對吧？

S : That's right. Because you have a different voltage in the States you need a transformer along with it... This one will do. It's $600.

對的。因為美國的電壓和這兒不一樣，您還需要一個變壓器來配合…這一個可以，六百元。

C : O.K. Let me have that, too.

好吧。我也買了。

S : Certainly. Is that all, sir?

當然。就這些嗎，先生？

C : Yes, I think so. How much do I owe you for everything?

我想是的。這全部我該付你多少？

S : It's 2,800 altogether.

總共是二千八百元。

C : Can you give me any discount?

能不能算便宜點？

S : I'm sorry, but we can't.

對不起，不能降價了。

C : O.K.... Here you go. 好吧…錢在這兒。

Useful Examples
————————————活用例句→≪≪≪·≪≪≪

① *It's made of plastics.* 它是塑膠做的。

② It will *kill* the toy soon. 它會使玩具壽命減短。

③ It is popular *throughout the world.*
　　它風行全世界。

④ It's *short for* nickel. 它缺少鎳。

【註】━━━━━━━━━━━━━━━◆◆

battery〔'bætərɪ〕*n.* 電池　　lever〔'lɛvɚ, 'livɚ〕*n.* 槓桿

transmitter〔træns'mɪtɚ〕*n.* 發報機

receiver〔rɪ'sivɚ〕*n.* 接收機　　function〔'fʌŋkʃən〕*n.* 作用；功能

universal〔,junə'vɝsl〕*adj.* 一般的；全世界的

standard〔'stændɚd〕*n.* 標準　　recharge〔ri'tʃɑrdʒ〕*v.* 再充電；再裝填

nickel〔'nɪkl〕*n.* 鎳　　cadmium〔'kædmɪəm〕*n.* 鎘

charger〔'tʃɑrdʒɚ〕*n.* 充電器　　bothersome〔'bɑðəsəm〕*adj.* 引起麻煩的

voltage〔'voltɪdʒ〕*n.* 電壓；伏特數

genius〔'dʒinjəs〕*n.* 天才

transformer〔træns'fɔrmɚ〕*n.* 變壓器

discount〔'dɪskaʊnt〕*n.* 折扣

How about something like a kimono?

禮品專櫃

<會話實況>

　　觀光客每到一地，必定對當地的**紀念品**極感興趣，尤其是極具地方風味、造工又精緻的產品，更讓人愛不釋手。他們常說：*I'm looking for a souvenir.* 我想買個紀念品。

Dialogue 1

S : Good afternoon, sir. 先生，午安。

C : *I'm looking for a souvenir for my daughter.*
　　我想買一個紀念品送給我女兒。

S : How old is she? 她多大了？

C : Five. 五歲。

S : *How about something like a Kimono?* We have Happi coats, too. It's a short-waisted, jacket-type of kimono.
　　買一件和服如何？我們還有哈皮外套。是一種短腰身、夾克型的和服。

C : Well, the Kimono *sounds more fascinating to me.*
　　嗯，和服聽起來比較吸引我。

S : Certainly. What kind of material would you like? We have cotton and polyester.
　　好的。您喜歡哪一種質料？我們有棉布和伸縮尼龍的。

C : Cotton's fine. 我要棉布的。

S : Here's one. There are *a couple of strings* connected to it,
so you can tie it up in the front. This one is $1,200.
And how would you like a belt with it? It makes it look
very nice.

這裏有一件。上面繫有一對細繩，可以綁在前面的。這件要一千
兩百元。您要不要一條搭配的皮帶？會很好看的。

C : O.K. Then I'll take a red one with it.

好。我要買條紅色的。

S : Thank you. It's $1,500 altogether. Although it is machine-
washable, it is better to wash it in cold water, not *luke-
warm* water, and *iron it later on.*

謝謝您。總共一千五百元。這件衣服雖然可以用洗衣機洗，但最
好用冷水洗，不要用溫水洗，然後過一會兒再熨燙。

C : I see. Thanks. 我知道了。謝謝。

S : Just a moment, please.... I'm sorry to have kept you
waiting. Here's your change of $500, and your receipt.

請等一下……抱歉讓您久等了。這是找您的錢，五百元，還有您
的收據。

C : I want some post cards, too... How much are these *a set*?

我還要買一些明信片……這些一套多少錢？

S : $90, sir. 九十元，先生。

C : *Where do you have stamps*? 哪裏有賣郵票？

S : At the Cigarette Department on the first floor.

在一樓的香煙部門。

C : O.K. Here you go, and thanks a lot.

好的，錢在這兒，眞謝謝你了。

S : Thank you. Please come again.

謝謝，請下次再來。

Useful Examples
———————————活用例句→◄◄◄◄◄◄

① I think it's an *ideal* souvenir.
   我覺得這是最佳的紀念品。

② It will be *a good memento of your trip* to Taiwan.
   這是您台灣之行的最佳紀念品。

③ All these purchases *make a pretty large parcel.*
   您買的東西很佔行李空間。

④ The chi-pao has been *the traditional Chinese costume*
   from the Ching Dynasty.
   旗袍自清代以來已經成爲中國的傳統服飾。

【註】————————————◆◆

kimono〔kə'monə, -no〕*n.* 日本和服

fascinating〔'fæsn̩,etɪŋ〕*adj.* 吸引人的

material〔mə'tɪrɪəl〕*n.* 材料；布料

lukewarm〔'luk'wɔrm,'lɪuk-〕*adj.* 微溫的

iron〔'aɪən〕*v.* 熨燙（衣服等）　*n.* 熨斗

ideal〔aɪ'dɪəl〕*n.* 理想　*v.* 理想的

memento〔mɪ'mɛnto〕*n.* 紀念品

parcel〔'pɑrsl̩〕*n.* 分配；包裹；一片

traditional〔trə'dɪʃənl̩〕*adj.* 傳統的；慣例的

costume〔'kɑstjum〕*n.* 服裝；劇服

10 How come the rate is higher?
滙兌地點

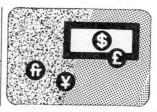

<會話實況>

　　向觀光客說明**滙兌地點**及**滙率**等是百貨從業人員最基本的待客之道，因此，此種有關業務一旦熟諳，百貨公司必會躋列國際水準之中，顧客盈門。例如顧客問：*How come that rate is higher for traveller's checks*？為什麼旅行支票的兌換率較高呢？店員就須詳加說明之。

Dialogue 1

C : *How come the rate is higher for traveller's checks*？
　　旅行支票的兌換率怎麼會比較高呢？

S : Because it's *guaranteed*.
　　因為它是有保證的。

Dialogue 2

C : I want to change only 25 dollars into NT dollars out of this.
　　我想從這兒祇把二十五美元換成新台幣。

S : I'm sorry, we can't do that.
　　對不起，我們不能這麼做。

C : Why not？
　　為什麼不可以？

S : Because we keep the number of your bill here, you see?
We have to tell the government *how many bills of what denomination are changed into NT dollars.* So, if you have a bill, here, *the whole amount* has to be changed into NT dollars.

因爲我們收了您的紙幣，您瞧，我們必須告訴政府多少面額的多少紙幣換成了新台幣。所以，如果您有一張紙幣要換，必須全數都換成新台幣才行。

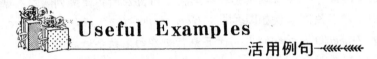

Useful Examples
活用例句

① I'd like to change these U.S. dollars into NT dollars.
我想把這些美元兌換成新台幣。

② It comes to NT$6,400 *at today's exchange rate.*
按今天的滙率折合起來是新台幣六千四百元。

③ *Would you like to change some money?*
您要滙兌一些錢嗎？

④ *We accept traveller's checks.*
我們接受旅行支票。

⑤ Could you change it *at a Foreign Exchange Bank?*
您到外滙銀行兌換好嗎？

【 註 】

rate〔ret〕*n.* 兌換率；價格
traveller〔'trævlɚ〕*n.* 旅行者；旅客
guarantee〔ˌgærən'ti〕*n.* 保證；擔保
denomination〔dɪˌnɑməˈneʃən〕*n.* 面額

貨幣專用術語

· 日　圓	yen〔jɛn〕	¥ , Y
· 印度盧比	*Indian rupee*	Re; pl. Rs
· 西班牙幣	*Spanish peseta*	Pta, P; pl. Pts
· 法國法郎	*French franc*	Fr, F
· 波　蘭　幣	zloty〔'zlɔtɪ〕	Zl, Z
· 美　金	*US dollar*	$
· 美鈔〔俗〕	*slang greenback*; **buck**〔bʌk〕	
· 英　幣	*British sterling*	
· 英　鎊	*British pound*	£
· 泰　國　幣	**baht**〔bɑt〕; **tical**〔tɪ'kɑl〕	Bht , Tc
· 捷　克　幣	**koruna**〔'kɔrunɑ〕	
· 港　幣	*Hongkong dollar*	HK$
· 菲律賓披索	*Philippine peso*	₱ , P
· 義大利里拉	*Italian lira*	L
· 瑞士法郎	*Swiss franc*	Fr , F
· 瑞　典　幣	*Swedish krona*	Kr
· 新加坡幣	*Singapore dollar*	S$
· 新　台　幣	*New Taiwan dollar*	NT$
· 德國馬克	*Deutsche mark*	DM
· 韓　國　幣	**won**〔wʌn〕	W

專櫃流行精品

- *Ready-to-wear* 成衣
- *Perfumes & Pharmaceuticals* 香水藥劑
- *Optical goods* 光學製品（眼鏡等）
- *Musical instruments* 樂器
- *Leatherware & Luggage* 皮件
- *Photo developing & Processing services* 沖印中心
- *Furriers* 皮草商
- *Handicrafts* 手工藝品
- *Fabrics* 毛（絲）織品
- *Household furnishings* 傢俱

- *Electronic equipment* 電器用品
- *Computers* 電腦
- *Supermarkets* 超級市場
- *Candy Shop* 糖菓店
- *Crystal & Glassware* 水晶玻璃
- *Antiques & Works of Art* 古董藝品
- *Brassware & Pewterware* 銅器白鑞
- *Souvenirs & Gift* 紀念品；禮品
- *Sporting Goods* 體育用品
- *Carpets & Rugs* 地毯；毛氈

附　　錄

百貨日用品一覽表
商店用語

附　錄

百貨日用品一覽表

《衣飾》

✦有襯裏的外衣	*lined garment*
✦大　　衣	overcoat〔'ovɚ,kot〕
✦腰　　帶	sash〔sæʃ〕, belt〔bɛlt〕
✦繫上腰帶	*sash clothe* , *sash bustle*
✦浴　　帽	*bathing cap*
✦髮　　飾	*hair ornament*
✦披　　肩	shawl〔ʃɔl〕
✦假　　髮	wig〔wɪg〕
✦小假髮辮	hairpiece〔'hɛr,pis〕
✦裝飾的髮夾	*ornamental hairpin*
✦絲　織　品	*silk fabrics*
✦毛　外　套	*fur coat*
✦珍　　珠	pearl〔pɝl〕
✦褲　　子	trousers〔'trauzɚz〕, pants〔pænts〕
✦吊　褲　帶	suspenders〔sə'spɛndɚz〕
✦象　　牙	ivory〔'aɪvərɪ〕
✦縐紗；縐綢	crepe, crape〔krep〕
✦手　　套	gloves〔glʌvz〕
✦長　內　衣	*long undergarment*

✦ 領　帶	necktie〔'nɛk,taɪ〕, tie〔taɪ〕
✦ 蝶形領結	*bow tie*
✦ 睡　衣	pajamas〔pə'dʒæməs〕, *night gown*
✦ 內　衣	underwear〔'ʌndə,wɛr〕,
	undershirt〔'ʌndə,ʃɜt〕
✦ 束　腹	*a stomach band*
✦ 活動衣領	*replaceable neckband*
✦ 短　褲	shorts〔ʃɔrts〕, trunks〔'trʌnks〕
✦ 短袖襯衫	*short-sleeved shirt*
✦ 翡翠；玉	jade〔dʒed〕
✦ 衣服質料；布	*dress material*, cloth〔klɔθ〕
✦ 棉製天鵝絨	velveteen〔,vɛlvə'tin〕
✦ 有邊的帽子	hat〔hæt〕
✦ 無邊的帽子	cap〔kæp〕
✦ 外　出　服	*visiting dress*
✦ 連身的袍子	*one-piece sach*
✦ 泳　裝	*swim suit*
✦ 紫　水　晶	amethyst〔'æməθɪst〕
✦ 浴　衣	*bathing gown*
✦ 圍　兜	bib〔bɪb〕, pinafore〔'pɪnə,for〕
✦ 衣　領	collar〔'kɑlə〕
✦ 尾部；底部	hem〔hɛm〕, bottom〔bɑtəm〕,
	trail〔trel〕
✦ 袖　口	cuffs〔kʌfs〕
✦ 袖　長	*the length of a sleeve*

✦ 襯　　裏　　　　　　lining [ˈlaɪnɪŋ]

《 日常用品 》

✦ 複製的鑰匙　　　　*duplicate key*

✦ 鉤　　針　　　　　*knitting-needle*

✦ 棒　　針　　　　　*knitting pin*

✦ 打的工具　　　　　beater [ˈbitɚ]

✦ 線　　　　　　　　thread [θrɛd]，yarn [jɑrn]

✦ 線　　軸　　　　　spool [spul]，bobbin [ˈbɑbɪn]

✦ 盆；罐　　　　　　pot [pɑt]

✦ 茶　　碟　　　　　saucer [ˈsɔsɚ]

✦ 嬰　兒　車　　　　stroller [ˈstrolɚ]，*baby buggy*

✦ 漆　　器　　　　　*japan ware*

✦ 尿　　布　　　　　diaper [ˈdaɪəpɚ]

✦ 手　電　筒　　　　flashlight [ˈflæʃˌlaɪt]，*electric torch*

✦ 火　　爐　　　　　burner [ˈbɝnɚ]

✦ 煖　　爐　　　　　stove [stov]

✦ 壁　　紙　　　　　wallpaper [ˈwɔlˌpepɚ]

✦ 開　罐　器　　　　*can opener ， tin opener*

✦ 溫　度　計　　　　thermometer [θəˈmɑmətɚ]

✦ 乾　電　池　　　　battery [ˈbætərɪ] (= *dry cell*)

✦ 噴　霧　器　　　　spray [spre]，sprayer [ˈspreɚ]，
　　　　　　　　　　atomizer [ˈætəmˌaɪzɚ]

　✦ 釘　　子　　　　nail [nel]

✦ 密　齒　梳　　　　comb [kom]，toothcomb [ˈtuθˌkom]

✦ 烤　肉　叉　　　　　spit〔spɪt〕, skewer〔skjuɚ〕

✦ 垃　圾　桶　　　　　*waste-basket* , *trash-can*

✦ 鞋　　帶　　　　　　shoelace〔'ʃu,les〕,

　　　　　　　　　　　　shoestring〔'ʃu,strɪŋ〕

✦ 鞋　　拔　　　　　　shoehorn〔'ʃu,hɔrn〕

✦ 輪　　椅　　　　　　wheelchair〔'hwil'tʃɛr〕

✦ 毛　　線　　　　　　worsted〔'wʊstɪd〕, *woolen yarn*

✦ 化　粧　台　　　　　dresser〔'drɛsɚ〕

✦ 香　　爐　　　　　　censer〔'sɛnsɚ〕, *incense burner*

✦ 冰鉗；冰夾子　　　　*ice tongs*

✦ 裝硬幣的錢袋　　　　*coin purse*

✦ 裁　縫　箱　　　　　*sewing box* , *sewing basket*

✦ 茶　　具　　　　　　tea-things〔'ti,θɪŋz〕

✦ 景　泰　藍　　　　　cloisonne〔,klɔɪzə'ne〕

✦ 皮　　包　　　　　　pocketbook〔'pɑkɪt,bʊk〕,

　　　　　　　　　　　　wallet〔'wɑlɪt〕

✦ 地　　毯　　　　　　rug〔rʌg〕, carpet〔'kɑrpɪt〕

✦ 種　　子　　　　　　seed〔sid〕

✦ 滅　火　器　　　　　*fire extinguisher*

✦ 公　事　包　　　　　attaché〔ə'tæʃə〕, *brief case*

✦ 沙　　漏　　　　　　sandglass〔'sænd,glæs〕,

　　　　　　　　　　　　hourglass〔'aʊr,glæs〕

✦ 有抽屜的衣櫃　　　　commode〔kə'mod〕, *chest of drawers*

✦ 清　潔　劑　　　　　detergent〔dɪ'tɝdʒənt〕,

　（洗衣粉）　　　　　*cleaning material*,（*washing powder*）

✦ 摺　　扇	fan〔fæn〕, *folding fan*
✦ 洗 衣 機	*washing machine*
✦ 陶　　瓷	china〔tʃaɪnə〕
✦ 開 罐 器	corkscrew〔'kɔrkskru〕, *cap opener*
✦ 電 風 扇	*electric fan*
✦ 日本草鞋	*Japanese sandals*
✦ 竹 製 品	*bamboo work*
✦ 壁 爐 架	fireplace〔'faɪr,ples〕,
	mantelpiece〔'mæntḷ,pis〕
✦ 茶　　托	*tea-cup holder*
✦ 飯　　碗	*rice bowl*
✦ 燈　　籠	lantern〔'læntən〕
✦ 畚　　箕	dustpan〔'dʌst,pæn〕
✦ 簾；帳	screen〔skrin〕
✦ 瓶	jar〔dʒɑr〕, pot〔pɑt〕
✦ 牙　　籤	toothpick〔'tuθ,pɪk〕
✦ 指 甲 剪	*nail chippers*, *nail scissors*
✦ 指 甲 銼	*nail file*
✦ 電 熨 斗	*electric iron*
✦ 電　　鍋	*electric rice-cooker*
✦ 燈　　泡	*light bulb*
✦ 桌　　燈	*desk-lamp*
✦ 眞空吸塵器	*vacuum cleaner*
✦ 電　　毯	*electric blanket*
✦ 陶　　器	earthenware〔'ɝθən,wɛr〕

✦ 腕錶；手錶　　　　　*wrist watch*

✦ 桌　　鐘　　　　　　*table clock*

✦ 錶　　　　　　　　　watch〔watʃ〕

✦ 壁　　鐘　　　　　　*wall clock*

✦ 鬧　　鐘　　　　　　*alarm*〔əˈlɑrm〕(= *alarm clock*)

✦ 衣櫥（衣服）　　　　wardrobe〔ˈwɔrd,rob〕

✦ 碗　　櫥　　　　　　cupboard〔ˈkʌbəd〕

✦ 污　水　槽　　　　　sink〔sɪŋk〕

✦ 平　底　鍋　　　　　pan〔pæn〕

✦ 鍋（較深）　　　　　pot〔pɑt〕

✦ 鍋　　蓋　　　　　　potlid〔ˈpɑtlɪd〕

✦ 螺　旋　釘　　　　　screw〔skru〕

✦ 螺絲起子　　　　　　*screw clamp*

✦ 煙　灰　缸　　　　　ashtray〔ˈæʃ,tre〕

✦ 秤　　　　　　　　　balance〔ˈbæləns〕, scale〔skel〕,

　　　　　　　　　　　weighing machine

✦ 剪　　刀　　　　　　scissors〔ˈsɪzəz〕

✦ 筷　　子　　　　　　chopsticks〔ˈtʃɑp,stɪks〕

✦ 針　　　　　　　　　needle〔ˈnidl̩〕

✦ 陽　　傘　　　　　　parasol〔ˈpærə,sɔl〕

✦ 抹布；餐巾　　　　　dishcloth〔ˈdɪʃ,klɔθ〕, napkin〔ˈnæpkɪn〕

✦ 床罩；床單　　　　　quilt〔kwɪlt〕,

　　　　　　　　　　　counterpane〔ˈkaʊntə,pen〕

✦ 床　　墊　　　　　　mattress〔ˈmætrɪs〕

✦ 軟毛被；羽毛被　　　*quilt of down, feather quilt*

+ 部　分　　　　　parts〔pɑrts〕
+ 腳　凳　　　　　footstool〔'fʊt,stul〕
+ 簾　　　　　　　shade〔ʃed〕, blind〔blaɪnd〕
+ 篩　　　　　　　sieve〔sɪv〕
+ 浴　袍　　　　　*wrapping cloth*
+ 床單；床罩　　　bedspread〔'bɛd,prɛd〕
+ 掃　帚　　　　　broom〔brum〕, besom〔'bizəm〕
+ 包　裝　紙　　　*wrapping paper*, *packing paper*
+ 餐　刀　　　　　*kitchen knife*
+ 奶　瓶　　　　　*a nursing bottle*
+ 盤　　　　　　　tray〔tre〕, salver〔'sælvɚ〕
+ 枕　頭　　　　　pillow〔'pɪlo〕
+ 枕　套　　　　　*pillow case*
+ 砧　板　　　　　*chopping board*
+ 熱　水　瓶　　　thermos〔'θɝməs〕, *vacuum bottle*
+ 飾針；大頭針　　*marking pin*
+ 縫　紉　機　　　*sewing machine*
+ 水　壺　　　　　pitcher〔'pɪtʃɚ〕, *water jug*
+ 蒸氣壺；蒸氣鍋　*steam kettle*
+ 焙盤；瓦蒸鍋　　casserole〔'kæsə,rol〕
+ 烤　架　　　　　grill〔grɪl〕
+ 冰　箱　　　　　refrigerator〔rɪ'frɪdʒə,retɚ〕,
　　　　　　　　　fridge〔frɪdʒ〕
+ 冷藏器；冰箱　　freezer〔'frizɚ〕

《 文具及其他 》

+ 紙　　板　　　　　cardboard 〔'kɑrd,bord〕,
　　　　　　　　　　pasteboard 〔'pest,bord〕

+ 油畫顏料　　　　　*oil paint* , *oil colors*

+ 色　　筆　　　　　*colored pencil*

+ 有圖畫的風箏　　　*picture kite*

+ 有圖畫的明信片　　*picture postcard*

+ 削鉛筆機　　　　　*pencil sharpener*

+ 音　樂　盒　　　　*music box*

+ （書畫用）立軸　　*hanging scroll*

+ 刀；劍　　　　　　sword 〔sord；sɔrd〕

+ 圖　　釘　　　　　thumbtack 〔'θʌm,tæk〕, *drawing pin*

+ 壁　　飾　　　　　*wall tapestry*

+ 紙　　夾　　　　　*paper holder* , *paper clip*

+ 砂　　紙　　　　　sandpaper 〔'sænd,pepɚ〕, *emery paper*

+ 橡　　皮　　　　　eraser 〔ɪ'resɚ〕

+ 顯　微　鏡　　　　microscope 〔'maɪkrə,skop〕

+ 西洋棋盤　　　　　checkerboard 〔'tʃɛkɚ,bord〕

+ 陀　　螺　　　　　top 〔tɑp〕

+ 書　　籤　　　　　bookmarker 〔'bʊk,mɑrkɚ〕

+ 朱紅色印泥　　　　*vermilion ink pad*

+ 水彩（顏料）　　　*water-color paints* , *water colors*

+ 西洋雙陸棋戲　　　backgammon 〔'bæk,gæmən〕

+ 墨　　汁　　　　　*India ink*

+ 墨　　　　　　　　*India ink stick*

✦ 雙目望遠鏡	binoculars 〔baɪ'nɑkjələz〕
✦ 算　盤	abacus 〔'æbəkəs〕,
	soroban 〔'sɔrə,bɑn〕
✦ 地　球　儀	globe 〔glob〕
✦ 色紙；日本花紙	(color) **figured paper**
✦ 積　木	**building blocks**
✦ 計　算　機	calculator 〔'kælkjə,letɚ〕
✦ 樸　克　牌	cards 〔kɑrdz〕
✦ 香　囊	sachet 〔sæ'ʃe〕
✦ 黏　土	clay 〔kle〕
✦ 膠	glue 〔glu〕
✦ 烟　火	fireworks 〔'faɪr,wɝks〕
✦ 版　畫	woodprint 〔'wʊd,prɪnt〕
✦ 信　封	envelope 〔'ɛnvə,lop〕
✦ 風　鈴	wind-bell 〔'wɪnd,bɛl〕
✦ 笛	flute 〔flut〕, whistle 〔'hwɪsl̩〕,
	clarinet 〔,klærə'nɛt〕
✦ 毛　筆	**writing brush**
✦ 文　鎮	**paper weight**
✦ 望　遠　鏡	telescope 〔'tɛlə,skop〕
✦ 自來水筆	**fountain pen**
✦ 放　大　鏡	**magnifying glass**
✦ 名　片	**business card**
✦ 牛　皮　紙	**vellum paper**
✦ 橡　皮　筋	**rubber band**

✦ 爽　身　粉	*talcum powder*	
✦ 刀　　　片	*razor blade*	
✦ 懷　　　爐	*body warmer*	
✦ 草　　　藥	*herb medicine*	
✦ 煙　　　絲	*shred tobacco , cut tobacco*	
✦ 口　　　紅	lipstick〔'lɪp,stɪk〕, rouge〔ruʒ〕	
✦ 瀉　　　藥	purgative〔'pɝgətɪv〕,	
	laxative〔'læksətɪv〕	
✦ 化　粧　紙	*face-powder paper*	
✦ 化　粧　水	*face lotion*	
✦ 香　　　皂	*toilet soap*	
✦ 體　溫　計	*clinical thermometer*	
✦ 殺　蟲　劑	insecticide〔ɪn'sɛktə,saɪd〕	
✦ 香	*incense stick*	
✦ 除　臭　劑	deodorant〔di'odərənt〕	
✦ 藥　　　膏	plaster〔'plæstɚ〕, salve〔sæv〕	
	ointment〔'ɔɪntmənt〕	
✦ 塡　塞　物	stuffing〔'stʌfɪŋ〕	
✦ 雪　茄　烟	cigar〔sɪ'gɑr〕	
✦ 牙　　　膏	dentifrice〔'dɛntə,frɪs〕, *tooth paste*	
✦ 維他命丸	*vitamin pill*	
✦ 漂　白　劑	bleach〔blitʃ〕, *bleaching agent*	
✦ 繃　　　帶	bandage〔'bændɪdʒ〕	
✦ 胭　　　脂	*cheek color*	
✦ 眼　藥　水	eyedrops〔'aɪdrɑps〕	

附　錄
商　店　用　語

A

account〔ə'kaʊnt〕會計

accounting〔ə'kaʊntɪŋ〕會計；
計帳

addition〔ə'dɪʃən〕追加費用

admission free 免費入場

advance order 預訂

advertisement〔,ædvə'taɪzmənt〕
廣告

advertisement agency 廣告代理

agency〔'edʒənsɪ〕經銷處；代理
商店

agency commission 代理佣金

agency contract 代理契約

agent〔'edʒənt〕代理人；代理
商店

amount of stock 儲藏量

amount paid 支付總額

anteroom〔'æntɪ,rum〕接待室

appointed date 指定日期

article〔'ɑrtɪkl̩〕*n.* 物品

articles for special sale 特賣品

articles on display 陳列品

assortment〔ə'sɔrtmənt〕
各色俱備之物；雜貨

auction〔'ɔkʃən〕拍賣

automatic vending machine 自
動販賣

average price 平均價格

B

balance〔'bæləns〕差額

bank〔bæŋk〕銀行

bank deposit 銀行存款

bargain〔'bɑrgɪn〕交易；合同；
廉價品

bargain sale 大拍賣

be on sale 出售

be out of stock 無現貨；賣光

be sold out 售罄

bid〔bɪd〕*v.* 出價

bill〔bɪl〕帳單

branch shop 分店

branch store 分店

breach of contract 毀約；違反契約

budget 〔 'bʌdʒɪt 〕 預算

bulk order 大宗訂單

bulk purchase 大宗購買

business 〔 'bɪznɪs 〕 商業;營業

business guide 商業指南

business hours 營業時間

business license 營業執照

business policy 商業政策

business recession 商業蕭條

buyer 〔 'baɪɚ 〕 買主

buying agent 採購代理

buying in 買進

C

calculating machine 計算機

calculation 〔 ,kælkjə'leʃən 〕 計算

call 〔 kɔl 〕 呼叫

cancellation 〔 ,kænsḷ'leʃən 〕 作廢

cancellation of contract 取消契約

card 〔 kɑrd 〕 卡片

cash 〔 kæʃ 〕 現金

cash account 現金帳戶

cash down 卽付現款

cash on delivery 貨到付款

cash payment 現金支付

cash register 現金出納機

cash transaction 現金交易

catalogue 〔 'kætl̩,ɔg 〕 目錄

change 〔 tʃendʒ 〕 交換

charge 〔tʃɑrdʒ〕 *v.*委託 *n.*費用

cheap 〔 tʃip 〕 便宜的；廉價的

cheap article 便宜貨

check 〔 tʃɛk 〕 支票

chit 〔 tʃɪt 〕 帳單

choice goods 精選品

cloakroom 〔'klok,rum〕車站中之寄物處

close shop 關店

closing time 打烊時間

commission 〔 kə'mɪʃən 〕佣金;酬勞金

commission（consignment）sale 託售；寄售

commodity 〔kə'mɑdətɪ〕商品

commodity tax 商品稅

compensation〔,kɑmpən'seʃən〕
賠償金

complaint〔kəm'plent〕訴苦

congratulatory present（*gift*）
賀禮

consignment fee 委託費

contract〔'kɑntrækt〕契約

contract deposit 契約保證金

contractor〔'kɑntrækɚ〕立約
人；承包商

contract price 契約價格

cost〔kɔst〕①價錢 ②成本

cost of production 生產成本

cost price 成本價格；原價

consumer〔kən'sumɚ〕消費者

counter〔'kaʊntɚ〕櫃臺

counting〔'kaʊntɪŋ〕計算

current price 時價

custody fee 保管費

customer〔'kʌstəmɚ〕顧客

customs〔'kʌstəmz〕進口稅

customs declaration 報關;報稅

customs tariff 關稅表

D

date of payment 付款日期

deal〔dil〕交易

decrease〔'dikris〕減少

deficiency〔dɪ'fɪʃənsɪ〕不足

delivery〔dɪ'lɪvərɪ〕遞送

delivery charge 運費

delivery man 送貨員

department〔dɪ'pɑrtmənt〕
部門

department store 百貨公司

deposit〔dɪ'pɑzɪt〕保證金

destination〔,dɛstə'neʃən〕
目的地

details〔'ditelz〕詳細說明書

discount〔'dɪskaʊnt〕折扣

display〔dɪ'sple〕陳列

display stand 陳列處

domestic goods 國產品

down payment 定金

draft〔dræft〕消耗

drawer〔'drɔɚ〕開票人

duration of an insurance 保險
契約有效期間

duty free 免稅

E

emergency〔ɪ'mɝdʒənsɪ〕緊急事件

emergency call 緊急電話

emergency exit 太平門

emergency stairway 太平梯

employee〔͵ɛmplɔɪˈi〕雇工；
　職員

entertainment〔͵ɛntɚˈtenmənt〕
　娛樂

estimate〔ˈɛstəmɪt〕估價單

estimation〔͵ɛstəˈmeʃən〕預
　算；概算

*examination（inspection）of
　goods* 驗貨

exchange〔ɪksˈtʃendʒ〕交換；
　交易

exchange rates 滙率

exclusive（sale）agent 總經銷

exhibition〔͵ɛksəˈbɪʃən〕陳列；
　展示（會）

expense〔ɪkˈspɛns〕費用

extend the market 擴展銷路

F

factory〔ˈfæktrɪ〕工廠

fee〔fi〕費用

finance〔fəˈnæns〕財務

finished goods 加工品

firm order 穩固定單

fiscal year 會計年度

fixed price 固定價格；不二價

food stuff 食品

foreign exchange 外滙

forwarding〔ˈfɔrwədɪŋ〕運輸

free delivery 免費運送

freight〔fret〕運費

G

general agent 總經銷

gift〔gɪft〕禮物

goods〔gʊdz〕貨物

goods free of duty 免稅商品

goods ordered 訂貨

grievance〔ˈgrivəns〕苦況

guarantee〔͵gærənˈti〕保證；
　擔保；保證人

guarantor〔ˈgærəntɚ〕保證人

guide book（sheet） 指南

H

head office 總店

headquarters〔ˈhɛdˈkwɔrtəz〕
　總店

high-grade goods 高級品

holiday〔ˈhɑləͺde〕假日

house-to-house visit 挨戶訪問

I

imitation〔ˌɪmə'teʃən〕仿造品

indicated price 標示價格

indication〔ˌɪndə'keʃən〕指示

information clerk 服務臺店員

information desk 服務臺

inquiry〔ɪn'kwaɪrɪ〕詢價

installation〔ˌɪnstə'leʃən〕裝設

installation expense 裝設費

installation work 裝設工作

installment〔ɪn'stɔlmənt〕分
期付款

installment delivery 分批運送

insurance〔ɪn'ʃʊrəns〕保險

insurance slip 保單

inter-call telephone 內線電話

internal telephone 內線電話

inventory〔'ɪnvən,torɪ〕存貨
清單

invoice〔'ɪnvɔɪs〕發票

J

judgement〔'dʒʌdʒmənt〕評判

L

label〔'lebl̩〕標籤

large order 大宗訂單

lease〔lis〕租期；租約

ledger〔'lɛdʒɚ〕總帳

letter of invitation 邀請函

list〔lɪst〕一覽表

list of articles 商品目錄

living necessities 生活必需品

long distance telephone 長途
電話

long term contract 長期契約

lost and found section 失物
招領處

lost (missing) article 遺失
物品

lottery〔'lɑtərɪ〕彩卷；獎卷

lottery ticket 獎卷

lounge〔laʊndʒ〕休息室

low-priced (bargain-priced)
goods 廉價商品

M

mail〔mel〕郵件

maker〔'mekɚ〕製造商

management〔'mænɪdʒmənt〕
經營

manufacture〔ˌmænjə'fæktʃɚ〕
製造

manufactured goods 製品

manufacturing cost 製造費用

manufacturing process 製造過程

manufacturing technique 生產
技術

mark 〔 mɑrk 〕符號

market 〔 'mɑrkɪt 〕銷路

market condition 市場狀況

market price 市場價格

market survey 市場調查

marketing 〔 'mɑrkɪtɪŋ 〕市場

measurement 〔 'mɛʒəmənt 〕
度量方法

merchandise 〔 'mɜtʃən,daɪz 〕
商品

merchandise coupon 優待券

method of manufacture 製作
方法

method of preservation 保存法

miscalculation 〔,mɪskælkjə-
'leʃən 〕誤算

misdelivery 〔,mɪsdɪ'lɪvərɪ〕
誤送

modification of a contract
契約修正

money order 滙票

monthly installment 按月分期付款

multilateral management 多角
化經營

n

necessity 〔nə'sɛsətɪ〕必需品

net profit 淨賺

newspaper advertisement 報紙
廣告

no charge 免費

no charge for service 免費服務

non-fulfillment of a contract
不履行契約

o

official price 公定價格

opening of a store 開店

opening time of a store 開店
時間

order 〔'ɔrdə〕訂單

order cancellation 取消訂單

output 〔'aut,put 〕①銷路
②產量

overcharge 〔'ovə,tʃardʒ 〕
過高的索價

overpayment 〔'ovə'pemənt 〕〕
多付

P

paid 〔ped〕已付清的

paper bag 紙袋

part time worker 打工者;兼職者

pay back 償還

pay in 繳款

payee 〔pe'i〕受款人

payment 〔'pemənt〕支付

payment in advance 預付

payment on delivery 貨到付款

penalty 〔'pɛnḷtɪ〕罰金

percentage 〔pɚ'sɛntɪdʒ〕佣金;
折扣

period for special sale 特賣期間

person in charge 負責人

personnel department 人事處

place of production 產地

place of purchase 購買地

place of shipment 裝船地點

planning 〔'plænɪŋ〕籌畫

portion 〔'pɔrʃən〕一份

post 〔post〕郵件

postal money order 郵政滙票

premium 〔'primɪəm〕①保險費
②額外費用

present 〔'prɛzn̩t〕禮物

preservation 〔,prɛzɚ've ʃən〕
保存

previous engagement 預約

price 〔praɪs〕物價;價錢

price index 物價指數

price list 報價單

price mark 價格標籤

price range 物價幅度

prices fall 物價下跌

prices rise 物價上漲

prime cost 成本價格;原價

process 〔'prɑsɛs〕製法

processed goods 加工品

processing 〔'prɑsɛsɪŋ〕加工

processing fee 加工費

product 〔'prɑdəkt〕產品

production 〔prə'dʌkʃən〕製造;
生產

production cost 製造費用

profits 〔'prɑfɪts〕利潤

prosperity 〔prɑs'pɛrətɪ〕繁榮

purchase 〔'pɝtʃəs〕購買

purchasing power 購買力

Q

quality〔'kwɑlətɪ〕品質

R

ready-made articles 成品

receipt〔rɪ'sit〕收據

receipt of money 進款

receipt slip 收據

reduction in price 折價

reference number 編號

refined article 精製品

refund〔'ri,fʌnd〕退款

renewal of a contract 更換契約

repay〔rɪ'pe〕付還

repayment〔rɪ'pemənt〕退款

rest room 廁所

result of business 業績

retail price 零售價

rise in price 漲價

S

sale〔sel〕售賣

sale by bulk 整批出售

sale in advance 預售

sale on credit 掛帳；賒帳

sales bill 售貨單

salesgirl〔'selz,gɝl〕女店員

salesman〔'selzmən〕售貨員

scarcity of goods 缺貨

security〔sɪ'kjʊrətɪ〕抵押品；擔保品

select goods 精選品

sell at cost 以成本價出售

sell loose 零售

selling〔'sɛlɪŋ〕售賣

selling agent 代銷店

selling by the piece 成件售賣

selling price 售價

settlement of account 決算

shipment〔'ʃɪpmənt〕裝船

shop-front〔'ʃɑp,frʌnt〕店面

shopping〔'ʃɑpɪŋ〕購物

shopping bag 購物袋

shopwindow advertisement 櫥窗廣告

showcase〔'ʃo,kes〕玻璃櫃櫥

sign〔saɪn〕符號

slip〔slɪp〕傳票

sole agency 獨家代理

special bargain day 特價日

special bargain department 拍賣場

special sale 特賣

speciality store 專賣店

specific insurance 特種險

specification〔,spɛsəfə'keʃən〕
詳細說明書

spot goods 庫存

stand〔stænd〕攤子；架

standard〔'stændəd〕標準;規格

stock in hand 庫存

stock left 存貨

stock taking 清查存貨;盤存

stock-taking clearance sale
清倉廉價

storage〔'storɪdʒ〕倉庫；貯藏

storeroom〔'stor,rum〕儲藏室

substitute〔'sʌbstə,tjut〕
代替品

substitution〔,sʌbstə'tjuʃən〕
代替

surrender〔sə'rɛndə〕收回保險
費而解約

7

tag〔tæg〕附籤

tailoring〔'telərɪŋ〕裁縫業

take charge of 索價；管理

tax exemption 免稅

tax rate 稅率

taxation〔tæks'eʃən〕課稅

tax-free article 免稅物品

telephone〔'tɛlə,fon〕電話

telephone operator 接線生

telephone receiver 聽筒

temporary〔'tɛmpə,rɛrɪ〕暫時
的；臨時的

temporary contract 臨時契約

temporary deposit of baggage
行李暫存

term〔tɝm〕期限

*term for the settlement of
account* 決算期

term of a contract 契約期限

term of guarantee 保證期限

term of validity 有效期限

terms of payment 付款條件

trade〔tred〕貿易公司

trade sample 樣品

trademark〔'tred,mɑrk〕商標

*trading company（firm）*貿易
公司

trainee〔tren'i〕見習生

transportation insurance 運輸險

try on 試穿

trust〔trʌst〕*v.* 委託　*n.* 委託物

𝒰

under-production 〔ˈʌndə
prəˈdʌkʃən〕生產不足

unit-cost 〔ˈjunɪt͵kɔst〕單價

𝒱

value 〔ˈvæljʊ〕價值

𝒲

waiting room 接待室

wastepaper 〔ˈwest͵pepə〕
廢紙；紙屑

wastepaper basket 紙屑簍

weight 〔wet〕重量

wholesale 〔ˈhol͵sel〕批發

wholesale price 批發價

wholesaler 〔ˈhol͵selə〕批發商

work shop 工廠

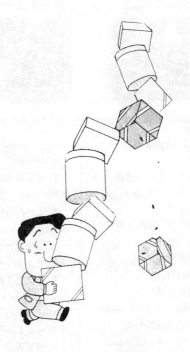

𝒴

year-end present 年終禮品

新一代英語教科書・領先全世界

學習語言以口說為主・是全世界的趨勢

店員英語會話

編　　　著 / 武 藍 蕙

發 行 所 / 學習出版有限公司　　☎ (02) 2704-5525

郵 撥 帳 號 / 0512727-2 學習出版社帳戶

登 記 證 / 局版台業 2179 號

印 刷 所 / 裕強彩色印刷有限公司

台 北 門 市 / 台北市許昌街 10 號 2 F　　☎ (02) 2331-4060・2331-9209

台灣總經銷 / 紅螞蟻圖書有限公司　　☎ (02) 2795-3656

美國總經銷 / Evergreen Book Store　　☎ (818) 2813622

本公司網址　www.learnbook.com.tw

電 子 郵 件　learnbook@learnbook.com.tw

售價：新台幣二百五十元正

2008 年 11 月 1 日新修訂

ISBN 978-986-231-003-8